The Party Girl

Kevin Whitaker

MCCLURE PUBLISHING, INC.
BLOOMINGDALE, ILLINOIS

2nd Edition

ISBN 13: 978-0-9915335-3-4

LCCN: 2015931842

Cover Design Image by: KREW ENTERTAINMENT LLC

Interior Layout by Kathy McClure
http://www.mcclurepublishing.com

To order additional copies, log on to:
www.mcclurepublishing.com
or call 800-659-4908

Table of Contents

DEDICATION

I dedicate this book to all students who are being mislabeled and discouraged. Never allow people to speak out against you. Your voice must be heard to protect your integrity and future. Be empowered so that all will know your story.

ACKNOWLEDGMENTS

First, I thank God for giving me this talent. Next, I thank my late Father, Quentin R. Whitaker, and Mother, Mae E. Whitaker, for teaching me to stand as a man despite the peaks and valleys of life. Last, but not least, I thank my family and friends for helping to make my life as interesting as possible.

In memory of my Godparents Annie and Gus Briggs.

WILL DO KREW, KREW ENTERTAINMENT GROUP, IVORY COASTS IMAGES, JOHNS LAW GROUP, PARKER TRANSPORTATION, Eminence Professional Educational Services, LOVE LEATHERS LLC., MAD CAPITOL CO., BUILDING BRIDGES CHICAGO, and THE TATE BROTHERS.

SHAIANNA NATHAN, BERNINA MCKINNIE, LEE STAGNI, ESTHER SINGLETON, MARY BOULWARE, MIKE GRIFFIN, RICK TAYLOR, J. BROWN, Dr. A. JOHNSON, CORY JOHNSTON, YOHANCE LACOUR(editor), KATHY MCCLURE(publisher), and NIQUENYA COLLINS (business coach).

Prologue

"The Party Girl" takes place in the City of Chicago at Curie High School. Alexis is a cheerleader and one of the most popular students in the school, whom everyone loves to hang around … despite her reputation for being the party girl.

Alexis has a crush on the star basketball player, Travon. His girlfriend, Janice, attends another high school. Alexis has decided she is going to make Travon her guy no matter what it takes.

This short story is filled with drama, deceit, suspense, action, and some sexual content … all with a realism that makes "The Party Girl" a must read.

INTRODUCTION

Coach Matthews calls a timeout to design a play for his star basketball player, Travon Singleton. As the players huddle in a circle, Travon nods his head in agreement and the play is drawn up. Billy Smith, the team's power forward, threatens to steal the moment if he touches the ball.

Knowingly, Coach Matthews reminds the team, "Hey, this is the time to show poise. There are scouts in the stands, so this is the time to show teamwork and run the play. And if we win this game, guys, we will be in the playoffs."

The buzzer sounds, and the team returns to the court. The center inbounds the ball, passing it to Billy, who waits for Travon to come around a pick with fourteen seconds left on the clock.

Travon comes off the pick set by the Condors' point guard, Carlos, at the top of the key. Travon is wide open and waiting on the pass as the clock ticks under ten seconds. Billy, reluctant to pass the ball, drives toward the basket with six seconds left, pulling up for a 15-foot jump-shot. Travon crashes the board, grabbing the rebound. He tips the ball toward the rim. As the time on the clock winds down, the ball catches the back iron of the rim, bouncing to catch the front of the rim before falling in for the score. The buzzer sounds. The game is over. Curie has advanced to the playoffs. The students storm the court lifting Travon in the air.

Billy mumbles under his breath, "Chump."

On the walk to the locker room, Billy and Travon exchange words. Billy had looked Travon off for the shot knowing that Travon was wide open. Travon is angry about Billy's shot attempt because Billy is a post-up player. A heated argument ensues with Travon throwing his wet jersey at the locker.

"You can't make a free-throw let alone a jumper! You're a hater!" Travon says.

Billy responds defensively, "You're not the only one who can make a shot!"

Coach Matthews interrupts, "Hold'em up gym-shoe. This isn't the last game. We made it to the playoffs, now see if we can win a championship! No more 'beef' as you all call it. Can't we all just get along?"

Carlos laughs, "Coach… Gym-shoe? Really? That's old school." The team laughs and Billy stares Travon down as everyone continues getting dressed.

Chapter 1

It's playoff time and the Condors are taking on their rivals, the Bengals. Coach Matthews has called a timeout to design a play for Travon with nine seconds left on the clock. The team walks back on the court. Travon returns to the free-throw line to complete his second attempt. The Curie Condors are now down by one point. The crowd goes wild as Travon makes his second shot to tie the game at 79.

The Bengals attempt a full-court pass. It's stolen by Travon. He quickly dribbles up the court as the time ticks ever so rapidly. He glances at the clock, pulls up at the top of the key and releases his jump shot. Everything goes silent as the ball travels toward the rim. The buzzer sounds. The shot goes in and the crowd erupts in cheers running onto the court to lift the team into the air. The Curie Condors have made it to the second round of the playoffs.

Coach Matthews yells, "Shower up and get dressed! We're going out to eat pizza. Home Run Inn!"

Benny replies, "Yeah, Coach Matt! It's about time you bought real pizza."

"It's about time you played like a real center," Coach Matthews fires back.

The team in unison, "Ohh!!! Coach treated you, Benny."

They all laugh as they walk out of the locker room in great spirits. The players' parents and friends are out in the lobby waiting to greet them. Everybody exits the building with most of the crowd going to the celebration at Home Run Inn Pizza.

The cheerleaders arrive before everybody else. Alexis takes it upon herself to reserve the area upstairs for the team. Coach Matthews and Assistant Coach Rob approach the second level to find the cheerleaders sitting patiently. People filter in. No seat is left empty. The dining area upstairs is packed with everyone enjoying pizza and chatting. Billy, Travon, and Carlos sit close to one another.

Carlos smiles, "Man, bros, y'all still on that nonsense?"

Billy grits his teeth, "It's on Travon."

"What's on me!?"

Coach Matthews notices the tempers starting to flare and gives both Billy and Travon a stern look. They both chill out to enjoy the moment.

Alexis is sitting with Lisa, Carlos's girlfriend, eyeballing Travon with a big grin on her face. She bursts out laughing every time she notices Travon looking in her direction.

Lisa cannot take it, "You're doing the most."

Alexis with a big bright smile, "I can't help myself. He is so fine."

Lisa jokes with Alexis, "Girl, you are gone. There's no hope for you at this point."

Benny and Billy chat on the low. Billy is staring at Alexis, "If that was my girl I'd treat her like a queen."

Benny looks Billy directly in his face with a dumbfounded look, "Man! A queen?"

Billy bursts out laughing, "Yeah, bro, for a day! Then I'd dump her!" They both laugh.

Benny ends the conversation, "She's still one of the finest girls in the school, thot or not."

Coach Matthews and Coach Rob stand before everyone. Coach Matthews asks for everyone's attention. Everybody keeps chatting in their little groups.

Coach Matthews yells, "All the ugly people keep talking." Instantly everybody gets quiet … except Billy.

Coach Matthews yells, "Yes, son, you are the ugly one." Everybody giggles for a second.

Coach Matthews states, "Billy you have the ugliest jump shot I ever seen."

Billy embarrassed, shuts his mouth.

Someone yells out, "TREATED!!!" People start giggling again.

Coach Matthews states, "Now on a more serious note, I would like to thank you all for the support over the regular season, but now it's playoff time," his energy level goes up, "I'm going to need more screaming and yelling and cheering until you can't talk anymore. Our kids deserve this chance to propel to the top bracket of the championship.”

Everybody hangs on to Coach Matthews's every word, “I'm not sure what you were doing this time last year? But this year we are shooting for the stars. Let there be no doubt that these young men have prepared for this battle all year long,” he pauses … “and now is the time to display your talents to your family, your friends, your school, but last and not least, yourself.”

Everyone has the eye of the tiger look upon their face as Coach Matthews closes out, “Let me thank all of you for the love and ongoing support, from the booster club to the scouts who come to watch our program to the fans. Now tell me who we are?”

Everybody screams in unison, “Mighty, Mighty Condors!!!!”

A couple of scouts, chat on the side. Coach Matthews knows how to get everyone going. One of the scouts, “Yeah, he had me going for a moment.”

The other scout, “Hell, we need to be scouting him.” They chuckle.

The scouts shake hands and depart. The crowd of people has started to disperse for home.

The next day at school, Travon is approached by Alexis in the hall locker area. Travon has always admired Alexis's beauty but considered her somewhat of a thot based on her reputation. She glances at Travon with a big smile as he's rushed off toward class by Billy and Carlos. Alexis Petitis stands there a little upset because they didn't acknowledge her presence.

One of Alexis's friends walks up to her, "Girl … why do you even bother with him? He's not even up to your standards."

"He is way up there," Alexis replies with a smile.

Sharon grabs Alexis's arm as the bell sounds, "Girl, please stop. You're doing the most when it comes to Travon."

"Whatever," replies Alexis with a smirk on her face.

Sharon and Alexis rush down the hall as Alexis thinks about how fine Travon is. They rush to math class, passing other students as the teachers start closing the doors.

"Okay students, the bell has sounded. Clear this hallway immediately," the math teacher states before closing the door.

Sharon giggles as she enters, "Girl … you almost made me late. I can't get another tardy."

"Oh well, you should have let me have my Travon moment," Alexis responds as they walk to their seats.

After class, Sharon and Alexis pick up their conversation in the hallway. It's passing period and the hallways are full of a diverse student body. High schoolers of all nationalities uniformed in red Polo shirts and tan khaki bottoms. Alexis becomes annoyed as Billy bumps her in passing, "Watch it!"

Billy looks back over his shoulder with a silly grin and keeps walking. "He such a lame," Sharon exclaims.

"He's irra … talking about he's white chocolate," Alexis said.

Sharon giggles, "Yeah right, who calls themselves that? Later Lex."

Sharon heads upstairs to class as Alexis continues down the brightly lit hallway with banners hanging celebrating the school playoff victories.

The principal of the school allows the basketball team to wear their jerseys the day after a big win. The spirits of the students were electric. Whenever they cross paths with one of the players, high fives and pats on the backs are given.

Chapter 2

The following week, the Condors play Dunbar High School for the City Championship. The Curie Condors defeat Dunbar 84-79 to advance to the State Championship.

Travon is the team's leading scorer with seventeen points and ten assists. Billy manages to get ten points and nine rebounds. Billy was upset that Travon had taken a rebound that would have given him a double-double, ten points and ten rebounds.

During the celebration on the court, Billy makes it clear that something is wrong, he never high-fives Travon. Travon is hugging all the players, family and friends. Carlos, Benny, Black Shawn, and Travon group hug as Billy stands back and watches. The four of them, plus Billy, make up the Condors' starting five.

Black Shawn, excited about the win, leans over toward Travon to try to speak over the celebration noise, "You know why Billy tripping?"

"No! Black Shawn, what's up?"

"That last rebound you got where you out-jumped Billy would have given him a double-double."

"MAN! This dude is petty."

Black Shawn nods his head in agreement, "I know, right?"

The players and coaches make their way to the locker room through the large crowd in attendance.

That weekend there had been a lot of parties scheduled and every one of them wanted Travon there. However, he has been invited down to a nearby college that weekend. The rest of the teammates had planned a big jam at one of the players' house.

Billy, a senior in high school and the tallest guy on the team, at 6'9", confronts Travon at a local gas station, "What's up?"

Travon smiles and greets Billy with a half-hug and chest bump, "What's up my dude?"

Billy, slightly irritated, "You, bigshot."

Travon continues pumping gas and looks up at Billy, "Huh? Dude, what are you on?"

"Nothing … it's you who never make the parties."

Travon returns the pump, placing the gas cap on the car, "Dude, miss me with that."

"Nawl, you miss me with BS."

Travon shakes his head in disbelief, "Every time I think we moved pass things you try to clown me. Dude, let it go."

"Yeah, all right … but I done told you I ain't your dude just because I'm white. My nig."

Travon flares up instantly, "I told you about that, just because you wear skinny jeans and listen to rap music don't get it twisted.

Billy replies sarcastically, "Yep you right," chuckling and turning to walk back to his late model truck, "Lame."

Music blaring, Billy pulls off, tires screeching.

Travon watches and slowly pulls away.

That weekend, Billy's uncle was hosting a party for the team. Travon went to visit a college with his mom.

During the drive, Ms. Singleton explains some of her expectations of Travon while in college, "Son, college can be a great experience. However, you can't lose track of why you're there. The parties, girls, alcohol, and drugs will tempt you daily."

She glances over at him. Travon sat there intently listening to every word his mom had spoken as she drove down the highway, "Mom, I know about the parties, girls, drugs, and alcohol. All that stuff is around the school."

Ms. Singleton frowns, "What do you mean? In the school?"

"Nawl, Mom. Around the school, kids know where to buy whatever they want. It's up to the individual not to partake in that type of activity."

She smiles, "Do you know where to get it?"

"No!!! I'm not into that."

"Oh, look, five miles to go before we're at the university," Ms. Singleton observes and then asks, "You excited, Son?"

He answers eagerly, "Yes!"

That evening at Billy's uncle's house, the party has begun. There are drinks and pills available with the latest hip-hop music playing loudly.

Billy walks around the house mimicking the lyrics to one of the songs. People just nod their heads to the beat. Most of the students who attended Billy's parties were C and D students who hadn't matured as young adults.

The D.J. plays a newly released hip-hop song, and the party instantly turns up. Billy, rocking the latest fashions, pants hanging off his butt, is in the center of the floor. Everybody gathers around Billy, bouncing, bopping, and pop-locking.

A circle forms as the girls battle the boys. Sabrina, one of the dance club members, steals the moment with her provocative moves.

Dennis, a freshman, takes the center of the circle moving like Usher. The crowd erupts in cheers. Billy's uncle sits back with his friends, who are all in their mid-twenties, watching all the young girls in the room.

One of the older guys takes a liking to Sabrina, a junior in high school. He whispers to Billy, "Who is that?"

"Who? Sabrina?" asks Billy.

"Yeah!" nodding his head in agreement, "I want her. Hook it up, dude."

Billy grins, "Don't trip, dawg, I got you."

Sabrina notices she's being summoned and walks over sheepishly, not knowing Billy's friend is the big bad wolf. He looks her over.

"Brina, meet Ty. Ty, meet Brina," Billy says.

Ty grabs Sabrina's hand, leading her towards him. She grins from ear-to-ear, liking the attention.

Over at the university, Travon and Ms. Singleton take the tour with the Dean of Admissions. He leads them to the cafeteria where there are other male students eating dinner with the basketball coach. Travon walks over to the table with the other students as the Dean makes an introduction, "Coach John, this is Ms. Singleton."

Coach John extends his hand, "Nice to meet you, Ms. Singleton."

"You as well, Coach John."

"I'll leave you two to your business," Dean Brown states as he walks away.

Coach Brown leads Ms. Singleton over to one of the tables where they chat awhile. Travon is laughing and having a great time with the students that are present.

Back at the party, Ty has Sabrina eating out of his hand with all of his fake promises. Sabrina, very naïve, just grins as he talks her into going into another room with him. Billy sees them going into the back room and nods his head in approval.

"Turn up!" Billy yells as the music continues to play.

Chapter 3

That Monday at school, after winning the City Championship and advancing to go down state, it's evident that Travon's popularity has grown.

Travon, standing in the hall during lunch period, is surrounded by students … mostly girls. Alexis watches from across the corridor becoming slightly jealous. She makes her way over to Travon pushing people to the side.

"Excuse me," says Alexis in a sweet soft voice, pulling Travon away by his arm.

"Whoa…. Where we off to?" Travon asks.

"To lunch. Don't you want to drive me to lunch?" She asks.

"I didn't drive today," Travon replies.

Alexis grins, "Don't be silly. I drove. You can drive my car." She tosses him the keys as they walk towards the students' parking lot. They approach Alexis's late model Mustang convertible and Travon's walk speeds up. Once in the car, Alexis blurts out, "Dang!!" while Travon is driving.

Travon, with a look of concern, "What's wrong?"

"You didn't even open the door for me. And here I'm thinking you were the perfect gentleman."

"Oh … that's my bad."

"I'm just joking," as she grins from ear-to-ear.

They sit in the car chatting as they eat their lunch.

Alexis turns the radio down, "Travon how long have you and Janice known one another?"

Travon sips on his drink and chokes slightly.

Alexis laughs and pats him on the back, "You okay?"

Travon clears his throat, eyes watering, "I'm all right," starting the car, "Janice and I grew up together before her parents moved out of the old neighbor-hood."

"Oh, I didn't know that" Alexis replies.

After grabbing something to eat they head back to the school and Travon's feelings for Alexis has somewhat changed since spending some time with her.

The next day during basketball practice, the cheerleaders practice at the same time. The teammates notice how Travon and Alexis make eye contact during both practices.

Benny, a senior and small forward, teases Travon, "Yo, Tray! I know you're not hitting that?"

"Man, hell no. But she's pretty cool," Travon answers.

Billy blurts out, "Yeah if you like thots!"

The team laughs!

Carlos, a junior and point guard, says, "She is fine, so I guess I like thots." The team teases him about his comment, "You crazy, Los."

Alexis looks over to the other cheerleaders and says, "They over there talking about us."

Tameika asks, "How can you tell, girl?"

"Because every time I look over there, they looking over here."

"Don't even worry though, I got your back," Tameika says.

Alexis looks over with a devious stare, "I know you do."

Practice is over, and everyone is standing around waiting for their parents to pick them up. The kids with cars are just hanging out with the team.

The cheerleaders walk down the stairs as if it were the Runway in Paris. All the guys turn to look at Alexis as she leads the pack. She moves right over in Travon's direction with the other cheerleaders on her heels, "So Travon, can you give me a ride home?"

"What happened to that fly ride of yours?"

"It's in the shop. My dad said it needed something. I don't know what that could be."

"It's cool. I got you," Travon responds.

Carlos admires Alexis's Coke-bottle shape, "Damn, she's fine…."

Benny interrupts, "Stop hawking, dawg. You're not in her league."

"And you are?" Carlos questions with a laugh.

Billy is salty, "Man, screw that thot!"

Carlos frowns, "Dude what's with all that negative energy? I can feel that all up in here," opening his hand and passing it over his face.

Everyone starts to laugh.

Billy mimics laughter, "Ha … ha … ha."

Travon pulls up on the side of Alexis's home on the corner of the block. Alexis leans over and kisses Travon on the cheek, "Thanks, Mr. Singleton."

"That wasn't necessary, but you're welcome."

"That was nothing," as she reaches over and rubs his thigh.

Travon moves her hand off his thigh, "You know I have a girlfriend."

"Yeah, what about her?"

"Alexis, look, I like you and all, but Janice is my girl."

Alexis's feelings slightly hurt, "So, friends it is … for now."

Travon firmly states, "No. Friends, period."

"Okay, friends it is," as she opens the car door and steps out turning around to catch Travon looking at her butt, "Oh, can you give me a ride to school tomorrow?" smiling, "my car won't be ready until tomorrow night."

Slightly embarrassed after being caught looking at her butt, he answers, "Yeah, I got you, friend."

She closes the door and Travon pulls off. She reaches into her Prada bag, removing the garage door opener and presses the button. The door goes up, and Alexis's car is sitting right there.

She smiles and walks inside, closing the garage door behind her.

Chapter 4

That Friday everyone is talking about the party of the year in the cafeteria. Travon and Alexis are eating at the same table with a few friends. Everyone at the table is eating hot cheese curls or cheese fries. Alexis has a plate of fries with mustard.

"That has got to be nasty," states Marshawn, a junior classmate who eats with them.

Alexis looks at Marshawn as she eats her next fry, "Mmmm good. Don't knock it before you try it," glancing at Travon.

Travon smirks.

Alexis removes another fry topped with mustard from her tray and feeds it to Travon, who is sitting directly in front of her at the table.

"Man! dude, that's gross!" Marshawn exclaims.

"It's not bad at all," Travon replies.

Billy shakes his head in disbelief, "Man dawg, are you a player or a lame? She got you eating out of the palm of her hand."

The table erupts in laughter.

Travon stares at Billy, but before he can realize what's happening, Alexis grabs his face, catching him off guard, and kisses him in the mouth.

Travon immediately pulls back, "Alexis…. I really wish you hadn't done that."

Alexis smiles, "Oh well, can't take it back."

Travon looks over his shoulder and sees Valarie, his girlfriend's cousin, who waves with an evil eye.

"Dang!" yells Travon.

Alexis had heard from Tameika that Valarie was Janice's first cousin and purposefully seized that moment.

The table erupts with disbelief, "Oh … yeah, that's what it is?"

Travon, upset that Valarie had seen what transpired, slides his chair back, "Damn!"

The bell sounds for the end of the period and every student jumps up to dump their lunch tray and head for class.

Later that evening, Travon returns home from practice. Ms. Singleton and Janice are at the kitchen table looking at fabric while she prepares dinner.

He walks over and kisses his mom on the cheek, "Hey, Mom!"

Travon, unsure if Valarie has called Janice, is reluctant to approach her. "Hey Jan," Travon exclaims nervously.

Janice, in a lovely sweet innocent voice, "Hey Tray!" Travon leans over to kiss Janice and she pulls away.

He ponders nervously for a moment.

"Boy, don't do that in front of your mother," Janice says.

"Sweetie, don't worry about me. I've been young before," Mrs. Singleton says.

Jokingly, Travon asks, "How many years ago was that?"

"It doesn't matter, because I'm not too old to whip your behind," replies his mother.

Travon rushes over playfully giving his mom a hug and kiss, "Mom you're still very young and beautiful. I can't wait to get to the NBA so that I can take care of you."

"Don't worry about me. Just keep those grades together. Everyone doesn't make it to the NBA. I'll be happy to see you go off to college. You're an academic student then an athlete. Those grades are most important," she gives Travon a serious look and he nods his head in agreement.

Placing the sample of material in front of Janice, Mrs. Singleton asks, "Now, what fabric would you like for your prom dress?"

Travon smirks, "You ladies go ahead and handle that. I have to study for an exam." He walks away, moments later he is stepping into his bedroom admiring the NBA posters on the walls. He stares momentarily and is interrupted by the sound of his cell phone.

"Hello."

"Hey, Boo."

"Who is this?"

"Alexis."

Travon moves quickly closing his bedroom door, "What's up Lex?"

"Everything is gucci with me. What's with you?" Alexis asks.

Travon looks eerily around the room as if Janice is standing there, "How did you get this number? And why is the music so loud?"

Alexis, offended, "Why you can't talk or something? I'm at Billy's uncle house we gettin' it in. Why don't you come over? I got the number from Billy."

"I don't think so. I got a quiz tomorrow."

Alexis pleads for Travon to come on out, "Please … just for a little while? PLEASE! Besides, be for real, who's going to fail you?"

Travon looks at the door to his room, expecting it to open at any moment, "Okay ... ok just for a moment."

Alexis, excited, "Okay boy, don't make me call you back because I won't stop calling until you get here."

"I'm on the way, bye."

"Good, I got something for you," Alexis replies.

Billy yells in the background, "Yeah boy … we about to turn up!"

Travon whispers, "Okay, where is the party?"

Alexis softly replies, "On Lamon at Rena's house."

"Yep, see you in a bit. Tell the guys I'm on my way."

"Okay."

Travon sits on his bed pondering his thoughts before walking to the kitchen where Janice and Mrs. Singleton are still sitting.

"Boy, where do you think you are going? Didn't I hear you say that you had to study for an exam?" Mrs. Singleton sternly asked.

"Yes, but I'm only going outside for a little while."

Mrs. Singleton firmly asks, "Why? It can't wait until tomorrow?"

Travon keeps his slow pace as he heads out the door, "I won't be long."

Before Travon can close the door, Janice asks, "You want me to ride with you?"

"Nawl, I'm cool," closing the door behind him. "You and mom go ahead and finish up."

"That boy sure has grown over the past few months. I'm very proud of him." Mrs. Singleton says.

"My mom and dad both say you raised him right," Janice replies.

Mrs. Singleton gets a little emotional, "I've done my best as a single parent."

At the party, music blasts as Travon enters bobbing his head to the latest hip-hop tune, slapping high-fives. He notices Alexis dancing in the middle of a group of guys. Billy, with both hands in the air, is one of the guys dancing over Alexis.

Billy ever so loudly, "Yeah BOI!!!!"

"Wow! You turned up in here," Travon states.

Alexis stares at Travon with the most seductive look, wearing the latest fashion, "Hey, Tray!"

Travon avoids direct eye contact with Alexis.

One of the guys passes Travon a beer. He declines, "Nawl, dawg I'm gucci."

Alexis moves closer to Travon, dancing with an unopened wine cooler. "Here, Tray, try this," as she opens the bottle.

Travon refuses, pushing the bottle away from his mouth.

"One sip of this wine cooler is not going to make you an alcoholic," Alexis says.

The guys chant, "TURN UP … TURN UP … TURN UP!!!!"

Alexis passes the wine cooler to Travon who succumbs to the peer pressure and turns up the bottle.

The party cheers him on, "YEAH!!! YEAH!!! YEAH!!!!!"

Travon consumes the contents of the bottle. "Now that wasn't so bad, was it?" Alexis asks.

"No, it wasn't, but that's not the point."

Before long, Travon is tipsy and dancing rather closely on Alexis's backside. She leads him away from the dance floor to a nearby room.

Travon slurs words, "Were … you taking to me?"

She grabs the back of Travon's neck, "Shhhhh," pulling him down to kiss him. The music could be heard pounding through the walls, but Travon's heart was pounding even louder.

Travon leans back, words slurred, "You telling me I came all the way over here for a kiss?!"

"No, you came to see me," as she turns off the light.

"Hey, it's dark in here…."

Travon feels the zipper on his pants go down. "Relax…."

Fifteen minutes later. Travon and Alexis return to the other room with the rest of the party. Travon grabs another wine cooler and a handful of Alexis's rear-end. She smiles, "Here's your gift."

He sips on his cooler, "Wow! You've done enough already," with a big grin on his face.

"Don't be silly," handing him the latest Smartphone.

Billy interrupts, "Boy, you're drunk?"

Travon's emotions get the best of him, "No one has ever done anything for me besides my Mom and Dad. Thank you!"

Alexis questions, "I know you're not about to get all sentimental on me? Boy, we gucci up in here, right?"

Travon looks at the time on his new Smartphone, "I got to leave this place. It just got real," thinking about Janice and his mom.

Alexis is surprised, "Boy, what are you talking about?"

"My mother is going to kill me."

"What?"

Travon rushes out the door with Alexis on his heels. "Tray are you okay?"

"I'm fine, just have to get home," speeding off.

Alexis yells, "CALL ME!!!"

Travon parks the car very quickly and jumps out. He pulls out his house key quietly, trying not to disturb Mrs. Singleton. He enters the room very quietly, closing the door ever so lightly when the living room table lamp comes on. He freezes in his tracks, "Oh, hey, Mom!"

"Don't 'hey Mom,' me! Boy, I can smell liquor all the way over here. I know you're not coming in here drunk."

Travon, sheepishly, "No ma'am."

"Son, I was sitting here getting all worked up about you after Janice and I both called your cell phone," walking closer to Travon, "EXPLAIN TO ME WHY YOU DIDN'T ANSWER?"

Travon drops his head in shame.

"That's right, Tray. Don't say anything, because Lord knows I'm trying not to lay hands on you," taking a deep breath, "All I have sacrificed to give you the things you want and this is the thanks I get? REALLY? Leave my car keys on the counter and hand over your cell phone."

Travon places the keys and cell phone on the counter. He reaches out to hug her, "I'm sorry, Mom."

She pushes his arm down and walks away. Travon gets a little emotional knowing that he just let his mom down. He slowly walks to his room.

Chapter 5

The next morning, Travon wakes with a headache and rolls over to look at the clock, "Dang!" Jumping up out of bed, he rushes into the shower. Brushing his teeth, he glances at the time as he stands in the mirror.

He throws on his clothes, gives himself a once over, and looks in the mirror, "Yeah, you on point." He runs to the kitchen and discovers the car keys missing. At that moment, the previous night replays in his mind, *what the hell was I thinking? OH ... I'm going to be late for sure now.* Racing back to his room he grabs the Smartphone Alexis gave him. He turns on the power pleading for it to be on, "Yes!!!" Quickly, he texts Alexis asking for a ride to school.

Alexis quickly responds, "I got you!"

Moments later, Alexis honks for Travon to come out the house. Travon shoots out of the house and opens the passenger side door. Alexis is in the passenger seat.

Travon is surprised, "Why are you over here?"

Alexis with a big smile, "Boy, stop with the games."

Travon is smiling from ear-to-ear as he pulls away, "Wow."

"Wow, what?"

"I have never driven a new car before."

"Yes, you have! When we went to lunch!"

"Oh yeah!"

Alexis reaches over and turns up the music. Travon has a slight headache and turns it back down.

In a joking manner, "Don't you know better than to mess with a Black person's radio?" Alexis asks.

"Yeah I do, but I got a slight headache."

Teasingly, "Oh … poor baby can't handle his alcohol?"

"I shouldn't have been drinking anyway."

"So you didn't have a good time last night?"

"I'm not saying that. All I'm saying is, I could've still had a good time without drinking."

Alexis is concerned, "I have the perfect cure for that. Pull up at the corner store."

Travon pulls into the store parking lot. Alexis jumps out of the car, darts in the store and emerges with two cups and straws. She pops open the trunk and fills the cups. She passes one to Travon.

Taking a big sip of it, he frowns, "What is this?"

"Your aspirin for that headache," she answers as she sips on her drink.

"My head is just going to be hurting. I'm not drinking."

"Okay, suit yourself."

"I see why they call you the party girl."

"Whatever!!! Just drive."

They reach the school parking lot. Travon turns the car off reaching in the back seat to grab his backpack when Alexis kisses him on the cheek.

Travon smiles and admires Alexis's beauty before getting out of the car. She steps out of the car, looking over the top, "That's it? You're not, not going to say anything?"

"Yeah, nice."

They both start to walk toward the building. Alexis walks closely to Travon, "Nice what?"

Travon laughs, "Nice car," and takes off running.

Alexis is on his heels, "Whatever, you hater."

He stops at the school, opening the door for Alexis as the late bell sounds.

In class, Travon can't focus with his headache mixed up with visions of Alexis's beauty. There is no doubt in Travon's mind that he has failed the test as he watches other students turn in their exam. He is sitting right next to Sharon.

She whispers to Travon, "Are you okay?"

Travon runs the palm of his hand across his face, "No."

The bell sounds and Mrs. Turner exclaims, "The remaining students turn in your exam, and this will affect your third-semester grade, and for those of you who didn't get the test done, may I strongly suggest you see me after school. Okay, you're dismissed except Travon Singleton."

Travon drops his head to the desk. Sharon pats him on the back as she leaves the room. Travon stands and walks to the teacher's desk.

"Okay, Mr. Singleton, why didn't you finish the test?"

Dumbfounded, "I just dropped the ball on this one. I'll be here after school."

"It would be in your best interest to be here. I don't want to report you to the coach."

"Yes Ma'am."

"Have a good day!"

As he enters the cafeteria, the lunchroom is loud with chants of, "Mighty ... mighty CONDORS." Alexis is leading the crowd.

Security steps inside yelling, "Hey ... hey, ... hey let's keep it down."

The room erupts with, "Hey hey hey ... hey hey hey!!!"

Security yells, "Okay, all y'all Robin Thicke fans. Be the first one to get sent home today. Now bring your voices down."

Travon walks over to the table where he usually sits with his friends. Alexis saved a seat for him across from her.

Everyone at the table is pumped up about the Condors going to State Championship when Carlos, the point guard on the team, asks Travon, "What's good, dawg? Why you looking like a sour puss?"

"Man, I just bombed on this quiz."

"How? You're a pretty smart dude. It couldn't have been that hard."

"Dawg, the topic alone threw me off."

Nina, a nerdy, funny kind of cute honor roll student, looks in Travon's direction, "If you need any help just let me know."

Alexis is irritated, "Thot, he doesn't need your help."

Nina, "I know you didn't call me a thot? You bust-down!"

"Whatever!"

At that very moment, two guys can be heard yelling across the lunchroom.

Chris stands from the table looking in Billy's direction angrily, "Where's my phone?"

Billy and a couple of other guys lay down a *stang*, passing Chris's phone off to one another. Chris gets up in Billy's face as security rushes in to defuse the situation.

"Give me my phone, chump," Chris demands.

Billy, both arms up in the air, plays stupid, "I don't have it, clown."

Travon looks over, disappointed in Billy. Billy laughs it up as the young man gets angry.

Carlos shakes his head, "One of these days someone is going to turn up on Billy and tap that ass."

Security removes Chris and Billy from the lunchroom and heads to the Dean's office.

Alexis not in the least bit amused by Billy's antics, "Anyway, what was the topic on, Tray?"

"It was on HIV and AIDS. After I saw some of the photos of little kids, I got stuck."

The table goes silent as everyone looks around at one another.

Benny blurts out, "Hell, if I get it I'm going to give it to everybody."

Nina responds, "It would take you to say something like that … you're just plain old ignorant."

Paul, one of the students at the table, questions, "Who gave you that topic?"

"Mrs. Turner," Travon answers.

Nina, with concern, "If you need help you know where I am."

Alexis, a little jealous, "He doesn't have the crap. Now back up."

Carlos leans forward, "I heard Mrs. Turner was a beast when it came to handing out assignments."

They all agree about Mrs. Turner giving tough assignments with simple head nods. The bell sounds for the end of the period and Travon stands to see Janice's cousin, Valarie, staring directly at him with an evil eye. They all exit the lunchroom.

Travon asks, "Hey Alexis, can you give me a ride home?"

"You had to ask. I got you."

After school, Alexis drives Travon home and drops him off at the end of the block. He walks from the corner entering the house. Mrs. Singleton is cooking dinner.

Travon hesitates before speaking, "Hey…. Mom!"

The home telephone rings before his mom can speak. He answers the phone looking at the caller I.D., "Hello."

"Yes, may I speak to your mother, please!"

"May I ask whose calling private?"

"No, you may not. Now put your mom on the phone."

Mrs. Singleton turns in Travon's direction, "Boy who's on the phone?"

Travon shrugs his shoulders, "They won't say."

He hands the phone over to his mother.

"Hello."

Mrs. Singleton says, immediately recognizing the voice on the phone, "Hey, girl! Oh, is that right?"

Travon hears the voice, but cannot make out the conversation.

"Yeah, these kids nowadays think they know everything like they started something new."

They both start laughing.

The caller shares something that she wants Travon's mom to address.

"Okay, girl, thanks again for calling. Talk to you later."

Travon tries to walk off as his mom motions for him to stay there, "Take care, bye." She hangs up the phone.

"So, why are you getting dropped off at the corner and whose car is that?"

Travon is puzzled, "Someone called you to tell you I got dropped off at the corner. Really? Where they do that at?"

Mrs. Singleton, sternly, "Who? And why?"

"A lady friend of mines from school," Travon replies.

"Okay, does she have a name?"

"Her name is Alexis, and we're just friends."

"I sure hope so. Janice has actually selected beautiful items for your junior prom."

"I know she has, Mom. Don't worry. We tight like two fat chicks in a phone booth," Travon blurts out in laughter, "ha ha ha."

"That's just wrong. You know better than to talk about folks."

He stops laughing for a moment, "Mom that's tight, right?"

He laughs until she gives him a hard look.

"Go wash your hands for dinner."

Travon returns to the kitchen and sits at the kitchen table.

Mrs. Singleton has a serious look on her face, "Son, let's talk about Alexis."

Travon smirks, "Okay."

"Is she the reason you have been coming in late?"

"No, Mom. I've been hanging with the team."

She stares him in the eyes, "Boy, don't start lying to me. I want to meet Alexis."

Travon chews on his food and pauses, "Okay. Enough said."

Chapter 6

The next day at basketball practice, Coach Matthews has the team sitting on the bench, "I'm expecting you all to be on your best behavior this weekend. I know some of you never been away from your mommies."

The team giggles.

"Like I was saying, been away from your mommies. But as young men, it's time to turn those breasts loose."

Carlos speaks out, "Yeah, Billy. Momma's boy."

The team laughs.

"Yeah, your momma's titty," Billy replies.

The team, "Oooh!!!! Kill'em."

Travon, a little more serious and growing irritated, "HEY! Listen up."

Coach Matthews regains control, "It's time to make your mothers proud. I won't accept anything less than your best," raising his voice louder, "NOW WHO ARE WE? WHO ARE WE?"

The team yells in unison, "THE MIGHTY MIGHTY CONDORS!"

"Okay, team! Arrive here bright and early tomorrow. Now hit the showers."

When the team returns to the gym area after the showers, Carlos sees Janice sitting in the bleachers. He nods in her direction, getting Travon's attention.

Travon is surprised, "Hey!" He walks up and hugs her.

"Hey," Janice replies, hugging him back.

They step away.

"Why the long face, beautiful?"

"I need to talk with you and didn't want to over the phone."

At that very moment, Valarie walks up, "Hey Stupid Star!"

Travon becomes worried. He wonders what Valarie has told her cousin about Alexis, reluctantly, "Hey, Val."

Janice hugs Valarie, "Hey girl!"

Billy, Benny, Carlos, and Robert walk over and greet them.

Billy asks, "What's happening?"

Carlos gives Janice a small hug because he and Travon are tighter than the rest of the guys.

"We going to turn up or what?" Billy asks, looking at Valarie.

"Hell no!" then very sarcastically, "How does it feel to be turned down?" Valarie asked.

"Treated!!!" Carlos yelled.

Janice whispers to Travon, "Can we speak alone?"

"Yes," Travon leads Janice away.

Janice sadly speaks, "You know that we never spend any time together since basketball season started. I was looking forward to going downstate with you. However, my dad said I couldn't go."

She drops her head, and Travon quickly consoles her, wrapping his arms around her, giving her a big forehead kiss.

She smiles, "Thanks!"

"For what?"

"Always being there for me."

She hugs Travon around the waist as he hugs her around the neck. They walk back over with the group.

Benny jokes, "Dang! It took y'all long enough. Is everything gucci?"

Travon replies with a smile, "We always gucci."

He kisses Janice on the lips as they all exit the gym. Alexis is upset about what she has just witnessed from behind the bleachers and is now convinced she needs to move faster to get Travon.

The next day, they travel to Champaign, Illinois, and back celebrating their victory on the bus. While singing the school spirit song, the bus pulls in the school parking lot where a couple hundred people are waiting. The doors of the bus open and the crowd erupts as the players step off the bus as if they were being announced before the game.

Mrs. Singleton works her way through the massive gathering and catches Travon's hands. At that very moment, Alexis makes her way over and plants a big juicy kiss on Travon as Valarie watches. Travon, caught up in the excitement, doesn't see Valarie.

Mrs. Singleton pulls him close and yells over the crowd, "CONGRATULATIONS, SON!!!"

He turns to his mother with so much emotion, crying and hugging her so tightly she also starts to cry.

Travon, in tears, "I wish he was here."

Mrs. Singleton is fighting her emotions, "I know baby," embracing Travon even tighter. She wipes away his tears.

Coach Matthews speaks in a mega-horn, "I'm going to need everybody's attention. QUIET PLEASE!"

Coach Matthews, standing on the bus steps with everyone's attention, "I know you know how hard this team has worked to bring this Championship back here. The cheerleaders as well did a great job."

Alexis yells out, "Squad!"

The cheerleaders all yell out, "SQUAD … SQUAD!!"

"Okay, cheerleader squad," Coach Matthews said.

Travon is still dealing with his emotion. Valarie makes her way over and places her hand on his back and whispers, "Congrats!"

"Thanks, Val."

"Now everyone must leave the school parking lot. However, there will be a big celebration this week," Coach Matthews continues, "Before we go, I need to hear it one more time. Who are we?"

"Condors!" the crowd responds.

Coach yells, "I can't hear you. WHO? WHO? WHO?"

"CONDORS! CONDORS! CONDORS!" the crowd responds as they start to leave the parking lot. Coach Matthews walks Travon and Mrs. Singleton to the car.

"Travon is quite the talent," Coach said.

"Thanks," Mrs. Singleton replies.

"I can't wait until next year to win it all again," Travon exclaims, fighting through his emotions.

Coach giggles, "Enjoy the moment first, son."

Alexis walks up behind them quickly in a soft tone, "Hello, everybody!"

"Hello, Alexis!" Travon responds, "Mom, I want you to meet Alexis."

Alexis extends her hand to shake Mrs. Singleton's hand.

"Nice to finally meet you," Mrs. Singleton says.

"Nice to meet you as well."

"I've heard about you dropping Travon off at home," Mrs. Singleton says, probing into the car situation.

"Oh, it's no problem? Right, Travon?" asks Alexis.

"Yes, it's fine," Travon replies.

"There's a victory party at Laura's house, I came to ask if you wanted to go?"

Travon looks at his mom. Without saying a word, she agrees to let him go.

Travon and Alexis walk off to catch up with the other students.

"Travon, don't stay out too late."

He nods back okay. Alexis looks back over her shoulder, "I'll have him back early. I promise."

Coach Matthews looks at Mrs. Singleton with a look of concern, "You might want to keep that young lady away from Travon."

Mrs. Singleton opens her car door and pauses, "Why?"

"She has a reputation for being quite the party girl."

Mrs. Singleton grins, "Really now? Last I checked all cheerleaders get that rep … even me. Or did you forget?"

"I'm just saying I hate for him to be led astray."

"Thanks for the warning, Coach. Good night!" She closes the car door and drives away.

At the party, Travon is walking around, and everyone is congratulating him on the win. The music is blasting and the whole school seems as if they're attending. The basketball team has a circle in the middle of the floor, dancing and celebrating as

Travon joins them. Travon kicks off a mini-dance contest in the small circle. Every time he makes a move, Karen tries to top it.

All that can be heard is the crowd cheering them on, "Yeah! Oh, get'em!"

A hand reaches through the crowd and grabs Travon by his belt. It's Alexis. She pulls him back into Laura's room. She is seizing the moment.

"Hey! Hey! What's going on?" Travon asks.

"Who did you come here with?" asks Alexis.

"You, but I was enjoying myself with the team."

Alexis locks the room door and pushes Travon back on the bed, "Enjoy me."

She dims the light as the music from the next room pounds loudly with some freaky lyrics from a late hip-hop song. She unfastens his jeans. He fakes resistance, letting her push him back. She looks deep into Travon's eyes, "Now this is how you take care of a Champion." She then gently grabs his manhood as she kneels down in front of him. Travon tenses up for a moment. His cell phone starts ringing but he ignores the flashing of his cell phone, caught in the moment. His phone keeps ringing. Alexis soon finishes what she set out to do. Travon sits up on the bed speechless.

Alexis looks deep into Travon's eyes, "Well, how was it?"

"It was all right." Travon, not wanting her to know it was only his second ever.

"Oh! It was just all right, huh?" Alexis asks with a smile on her face, "I guess I'll have to do better next time."

"I suppose so," agrees Travon, zipping his jeans with a big grin on his face. He pulls his cell phone out of his pocket to look at the five missed calls from Janice.

They ease out of the room and back into the party where the music seems to be even louder. Alexis and Travon split up. Travon makes his way around and sees Carlos standing with Janice and Valarie. His heart pounds as he tries to play it off by reaching out to hug Janice, "Hey Sweetie!"

Janice slightly upset, "Where were you? I've been looking for you."

Carlos blurts out, "That's your ass Mister Postman!"

Travon gives Carlos a mean look, "I went to the store with Robert."

"For what?"

"Some beer."

Valarie adds her two cents, "He lying, whatever!"

"I thought you said you couldn't come out?" Travon asks.

"I said that. I guess my dad got tired of me sitting up in his face, so he said, 'go and be with your boyfriend.' Then I get here and can't find you."

She reaches up to kiss Travon on the cheek. He grabs her fat butt and kisses her in the mouth.

Alexis, across the room, is furious.

Valarie looks right at Alexis, watching her cousin, "Jan, there go that thot over there watching you."

Janice, enjoying Travon, turns and glances over her shoulder, "Who Val?"

Valarie responds bitterly, "Alexis!"

Janice looks over in Alexis's direction and whispers to Travon, "She is cute. You want that thot?"

"Hell no! Everybody knows that you're my girl," he responds as they continue dancing.

Meanwhile, Billy has gotten pretty drunk and has begun feeling all over Alexis as he watches Travon and Janice.

Billy grabs Alexis by her tight jeans, spinning her face-to-face and starts tongue kissing her. She doesn't even put up a fight, pissed at Travon, giving him a cold hard stare while kissing Billy.

Billy begins jumping up and down, "Turn up!"

Chapter 7

That Monday at school, banners hang everywhere. Students begin slapping high-fives and fist bumps as they pass one another in the hallway.

Travon is in deep thought about Saturday night and what transpired between with Alexis when Carlos approaches quickly, "What's up Bro?"

Travon is nonresponsive.

Carlos yells, "WHAT'S UP BRO!"

Travon stares at Carlos, "Dang! Dude why you yelling?"

Carlos gapes at Travon, "Man, bro, where you at? I called you at least two times. Come on let's get to the locker-room."

They proceed down the hall with everybody passing and tapping them on their backs in a celebratory manner. In the locker room, Travon explains to Carlos what took place on Saturday night.

"Dang fool! You are the man," jumping up off the bench, Carlos stands over him.

"Man, sit yo butt down."

Billy enters the locker room yelling, "Turn up! We number one up in this PIECE! Yeah thanks to me."

"Yeah! It's been rough, but we got it done, not just you," Carlos responds.

Billy gloats, "Yeah … I think Alexis is feeling me now BOY! Now what?"

Carlos looks at Travon and bursts out laughing. Travon, with a blank look on his face, lets on that something is wrong.

Carlos stops laughing, out of breath, "Alexis is only into Alexis fool."

Billy, defensively, "Man Los, I think you a hater."

Carlos takes a little offense to that remark, "How wrong can I be about that 'thot' as you call her?"

Billy, with a sour look, turns toward Travon, "What you got to say Stupid Star?"

Travon just sits, not speaking a word.

"Now, back to Los with your hating ass. Don't disrespect me or my peeps ever, clown. You dig!"

Carlos stands to step towards Billy.

Billy, towering over Carlos, "How would you like if I talked about Lisa?"

Carlos is looking up at Billy, "Dude, Lisa is my girl. Alexis is not your girl, she's a 'thot,' right?"

Travon shakes his head and giggles, "Y'all crazy. Just stop with all the thot stuff. Really?"

Billy, angrily, "Los, get out my face."

Carlos is not backing down, "Or what? You tripping over one damn kiss? Bring my girl into this crap? Man, SCREW YOU!"

Billy pushes Carlos back with force. Travon steps between them. Carlos is the aggressor but Travon continues holding them apart.

"It's on and crack'n," Carlos exclaims.

"Turn up then … Turn up!" Billy replies.

"Turn down…." Travon says, holding them apart.

Carlos calms down, backing up off Travon, "Dawg, he shouldn't have put his hands on me. For real!"

Billy torments Carlos, "What you gonna do? Turn up then, clown!"

Carlos turns to Travon, "Tell him, Bro!"

"Don't even go there, bro," Travon responds ever so seriously.

Billy is curious, "What that chump talking about?"

"Ha ha ha… yo chump in your mouth," Carlos says with a big grin on his face, "what Tray penis tastes like, fool? You were all kissing Alexis after she B J Tray. Now, who got TREATED!!!"

Billy is calm but furious inside, "Travon is that how it went down, bro?"

Travon drops his head, not wanting to get involved, then nods reluctantly.

Billy is serious, "Okay, it just got real up in here. My own teammates played me? Got you! Both of you bitches going to get yours." He slaps the locker with extreme force.

Carlos laughs, "What happened to your Black accent?" mimicking Billy, "both of you bitches going to pay."

Billy is devastated, "So, Travon, what am I to you?"

Carlos is cracking himself up, "You still BJ too, and not Billy Jr. Ha, ha!!!"

Billy turns away furious, "Okay, then that's what's up. You fools going to pay."

Travon turns to Carlos heated, "Damn Dawg! Why you have to take it there? You run your mouth like a female dog, shut the hell up sometimes, DANG!" as he storms out of the locker room.

Carlos is sitting alone, "I ain't nobody's bitch!" he turns and punches the locker, "screw both of you."

It's lunch period and the celebration has begun. Coach Matthews has hired a D.J. for the party, and the music is pumping as if the Chicago Bulls are about to be announced. The coach calls names in a deep, loud voice, "Coming in at 6'9", playing center … Billy Wrigley!"

The gym erupts as Billy runs out slapping high-fives. Then, Matthews calls out the rest of the team, saving Travon for last. The lights are dim as everyone goes wild expecting Travon to be the next person to come out of the tunnel. The crowd is so loud that nobody hears the coach call Travon, but he appears as everyone screams, "Super Star … Super Star!" Travon runs over and joins the team taking pictures with the trophy. Coach Matthews passes the microphone to Travon.

"Okay … k … k … k!" Travon yells.

The crowd calms down to hear Travon speak.

"I want to thank God, my mom, the team, and my school for all the encouragement over the season. In closing, I hope you're ready for another next year!"

The gym explodes with cheers as the music starts and the students start to dance. Carlos and Billy exchange dirty looks as Travon watches both of them from a distance shaking his head in disbelief.

Chapter 8

The next morning, Mrs. Singleton is in the kitchen when Travon comes down still half asleep sitting at the table.

"Tray we need to have a heart-to-heart."

Travon is curious with a look of concern on his face, "What about, Mom? Success and women."

"Huh?"

"Let's just say I'd rather see you with Janice than Alexis."

"Mom, don't worry about Alexis. We're just friends."

Mrs. Singleton smirks, "Oh is that right? I see how she looks at you and you at her. I just want you to know Janice is more grounded and has a future. I don't know about Alexis to say what's in her future."

She and Travon continue to eat breakfast and talk.

"Mom, I feel you on that, but Janice is my girl."

Mrs. Singleton grins, "Good to know, Son."

At that very moment, Travon's smartphone vibrates with two text messages. One is from Alexis and one is from Janice. Alexis's message reads, CU AT SCHOOL CHAMP.

Janice's message is a reminder, HEY TRAY, DON'T FORGET ABOUT THE TUX FITTING TODAY AFTER SCHOOL.

Travon's big grin forces his mom to smile and ask, "And who got you smiling this morning?"

He giggles, "You, Mom!"

Travon gathers his things and proceeds out the door for school.

When he arrives at school, it is still a celebratory moment with all students in a good mood. He makes his way through the crowd headed to math class when he approaches Billy. He and Billy reach the classroom door about the same time. Billy blocks the door and Travon gives him a hard stare like, WHAT?

"Yo, Tray! We need to talk."

The bell sounds as Travon looks at Billy.

"We're about to be late. Can it wait?"

Billy, with a stern voice, "Nawl, Dawg. It can't wait."

Travon steps to the side of the door and Billy as well.

"I can't get that mess out my head Carlos said to me," Billy confesses, "and for real, Bro, that crap got me feeling some type of way."

Travon is curious, "So what are you saying? I told you I didn't mean for it to play out that way. I apologize."

"Yeah, okay! After I do what I gotta do then I'll apologize to see if it makes it better," Billy exclaims.

Travon pauses for a moment and with a little aggression, "And what's that supposed to mean?"

Billy smirks and walks into the classroom. Travon walks in class behind Billy, pondering on Billy's words.

That afternoon at school, students hang around the first floor to find out who has been named the prom king and queen.

Carlos, Benny, and Jimmy are sophomores but their skills on the court have earned them spots on the varsity team. All of the basketball players stand around waiting as well.

Carlos sees Travon coming toward them, "Yo Tray!"

Travon looks in Carlos's direction, glances at the bulletin board, and keeps it moving.

"What's up with Travon?" Jimmy asks.

Carlos turns away thinking to himself, *DANG*! Nothing, and says, "He'll be alright."

The principal walks out of her office with the names of the prom king and queen. She posts them on the board. As the students spread to let her out, they rush the board.

All that can be heard is laughter, crying, and the calling of the winners' names.

* * *

At the tailor shop, Janice is looking for a tux to match her beautiful dress. She notices that Travon isn't really into it. Travon is off in a daze when Janice walks over to him and asks, "Can I smack you really hard?"

"Yep," Travon replies.

Janice smiles then smacks him lightly.

Travon responds quickly, "What was that for?"

"You told me it was okay."

Janice laughs and Travon pulls her close to him. She blushes, "So why you're not into this? Is everything okay?"

"I just have a lot on my mind."

She kisses him, "What about now?"

"Nope, just you," he responds and kisses her.

She grabs his hand and pulls him over to the shoes.

Meanwhile, at the mall, Billy is with a few of his friends. They're talking crazy about chicks that pass by.

Then, out of nowhere, Billy, thinking about the locker-room incident, says, "I'm bout to turn up on these fools."

His friends are confused. One of them asks, "Dude, what the hell are you talking about?"

Billy, with the look of death in his eyes, answers, "Nothing."

Shawn looks at Billy, "Dude, what the hell you on? Let it go. You're killing my vibe."

"It's turn up time … they don't know me like that," Billy responds, nodding his head.

"Whatever, Dawg! It's too many chicks in here to be on some personal crap," Shawn says.

Travon makes it home from the tuxedo shop dragging into the house where his mother is sitting in the living room.

"What's wrong son? Why the long face?"

"Wow! Is it that obvious?"

"Come give me a hug."

He walks over and hugs her.

"Most parents know when something is wrong with their child," Travon's mom says as she kisses him lightly on the forehead, and before he walks away, "just maybe this will cheer you up."

Travon pauses in his tracks, "What's that, Mom?"

With excitement, she responds, "Carlos called and says that you were chosen for prom king. I'm very proud of you and the things you have accomplished."

"Woo hoo!" Travon shouts.

"Now go and get cleaned up we're going out for dinner."

"Mom, that's not necessary. You're already paying for my prom and Janice's prom. I appreciate it, but I don't want to put any more stress on you."

Her eyes fill with tears of joy, "My baby has matured right before my eyes at the same time it moves my heart that you're so thoughtful. I've worked all my life to see this moment. And what I'm saying is the Lord has brought us this far, we are going to be just fine. Get ready, Son."

Travon kisses and hugs her tightly then walks away to his room. He yells from his bedroom, "Mom, did Carlos say who won for prom queen?"

"He said it was Ms. Petitis."

Travon screams in laughter.

"Boy, what is your problem?"

"That's Alexis, Mom!" He giggles.

"Oh really," with a slight look of concern on her face.

Chapter 9

At the mall, Alexis, Samantha, Darlene, and a couple of other cheerleaders are shopping when they run into Anna and Nancy, good friends of Billy's from school.

Anna, always high or stoned, "What's up, chicks?"

Alexis responds, "Shopping!"

Darlene frowns up at Anna and Nancy. Wanting nothing to do with them, she slides away.

Samantha follows behind Darlene and says, "Darlene, those girls are tweaked out."

"Yeah right, it's not even funny," Darlene replies.

Anna continues talking with Alexis.

"Lex, Fat Freddie is having this bomb ass party. You think you'll come out?" Anna asks.

Nancy chimes in, "Yeah! He has the keys to one of his dad's vacant buildings."

"How does Freddie pull that off? I heard his parties be off the chain," Alexis responds.

Anna explains, "Freddie's dad is big on properties and what not. He makes Freddie clean them, and that's how he gets the keys."

"Real estate," Nancy says.

Anna giggles, "Whatever! It's the hot spot."

"I always wanted to go to one of Freddie's parties. Count me in," Alexis replies.

Darlene and Samantha shake their heads in disagreement.

Anna with a devious grin, "I'll text you the information. Freddie sends out his invites by text."

Anna and Nancy walk off laughing at Darlene and Samantha. "They some lames," Nancy continues laughing.

Darlene stares at them as they walk away.

"Them chicks are a hot mess," Samantha says.

"I know you're not serious about going anywhere with those tots," Darlene exclaims.

Alexis laughs, "Thots … girl, not tots. I'm going to that party. I know it's going to be cracking. Which one of you chicks are going with me?"

They both look at one another. "Not me!" Darlene says.

"Miss me with that one," Samantha replies.

As they walk away, Alexis speaks, "I guess I'll be flying solo."

Darlene is concerned, "I wouldn't be caught dead with them Stoners!"

Samantha is confused, "What does that mean?"

Darlene frowns, "They'll use any drug they can find."

"Oh, that's them, but I do love to party," Alexis replies as they resume their shopping.

Later that evening, Travon and his mom are eating dinner when Travon gets a text from Alexis that reads,

HEY TRAVON, I SEE YOU'RE A CHAMP TWICE. I GUESS WE HAVE TO CELEBRATE AGAIN PROM KING! CALL ME. I KNOW WHERE FREDDIE'S PARTY IS.

Travon has a big grin on his face that makes his mom ask, "Who got you grinning like that?"

Travon replies, "Nobody, just thinking back on something."

He responds to Alexis's text, I'M WITH MOM NOW, BUT I'LL GET BACK TO YOU ON CELEBRATING CAN'T WAIT TO SEE WHAT'S NEXT.

"Tray, put that phone away," Mrs. Singleton says strictly, "let's talk about women and the life of a young man on the rise."

They talk while finishing dinner.

Later in Travon's room, he's going over some homework when his mom enters with the cordless phone, "You have a call, Son."

Travon is confused as to why anyone would be calling the house phone for him. He takes the phone from his mom, "Hello!?"

A sincere voice replies, "Hey Tray, what's up? It's me, Billy."

Travon's eyebrows rise, "What's up, Billy?"

"I know where Fat Freddie's party is tonight. You should come on out," Billy says.

"Man, it's a school night."

"Bro, it's good. Come on out and Turn up!"

Travon, wondering what Billy's angle is, "Nawl, I'm going to pass on this one."

Billy sounds disappointed, "Oh well, this one you shouldn't miss. It's going down tonight."

"What's going down?"

Billy laughs, "You got to be there to see."

"Nawl, I can't make it," Travon ends the phone call.

Moments later the phone rings again. Travon, a little annoyed, "Hello!"

"And hello to you too, Mr. Singleton," says Janice.

Janice and Travon talk for over thirty minutes when his text alert begins to flash. The message is from Alexis, HEY! THOUGHT YOU WOULD HAVE CALLED BY NOW. OH WELL, OFF TO FAT FREDDIE'S PARTY. ANNA AND NANCY INVITED ME.

Janice is speaking without a response from Travon, "Tray! Tray! Are you still there?"

"Yeah!"

Janice, a little irritated, "I better let you go … seeing you're not paying me no attention."

Travon tries to explain, "I got a lot on my mind."

"Well, let me go. Bye!" Janice ends the call.

Travon immediately dials Carlos cell phone, "Answer!"

Carlos, with a Spanish accent, "Hellooo!"

"What you doing?" asks Travon.

"Making out with my girl Lisa."

"I need you to ride to Fat Freddie's spot tonight? What's up? You coming?" asks Travon.

Carlos is sitting on the couch with Lisa, "I don't mess with them dudes, period."

Travon, pissed, "Whatever, Mr. Big Mouth. I'm gone."

He texts Alexis, warning her not to go to the party, DON'T GO TO THAT PARTY SOMETHING ISN'T RIGHT.

Alexis, sitting on her bed at home, reads the text and keeps it moving as if she never heard from Travon. She makes her way outside to attend the party.

Chapter 10

At Freddie's party, the music is deafening with neon lights and glow-in-the-dark paint throughout the building. Alexis is dancing around having a great time with a group of people she just met.

She's really into the music. As it pounds, she does the latest dance, sweat dripping from her forehead.

Anna approaches carrying a bottle of water. Alexis pulls her hair back and wipes sweat from her forehead with her hand.

"Woo, girl, where are the real drinks?" Alexis asks.

Anna pulls Alexis closer, battling to be heard over the music, "The only thing you need around here is water," pulling a couple of pills out of her pocket, "here, take one of these pills. It will energize you."

"Are you going to take one?" Alexis asks, spinning around to the music.

"I've already taken two," Anna responds.

"No, I'll pass on the pill," Alexis says as she reaches for Anna's water bottle, "but I'll have some of your water."

"Okay girl, you can keep the water," Anna responds.

Alexis slams the water down her throat, drinking the full contents and continues dancing.

Anna turns to walk away, making eye contact with Billy who is standing over on the wall. Billy makes his way toward Anna and passes her another package.

He leans over to whisper in Anna's ear, "Did she take it?"

Anna with a devilish grin, "No, but she drank the water."

"That's cool. I put three pills in there."

Anna is surprised, "What? That's too much for her."

"Whatever! Get gone. You got what you wanted."

He turns and makes his way over to Alexis as she dances.

Alexis thinks nothing of it and spins in Billy's direction, dancing with him. Soon after, she starts to sweat profusely. As sweat runs down her neck, Billy's eyes follow those beads of sweat and moves closer. He touches her breast. Alexis keeps dancing as if she invited Billy closer, grabbing his waist, feeling lightheaded. Billy places his arms under Alexis's shoulder to hold her up. He thinks to himself, got this thot now.

Alexis is complaining about the heat, "It's too hot!"

Billy signals for Anna and Nancy to come over. They immediately came over. "Take her in the back room," Billy orders.

Nancy and Anna escort her to the back of the building. "Give her some cold water," Anna says.

Nancy, entirely against helping Alexis, "NO!" The door to a back room opens.

Meanwhile, Travon is searching for the party. He keeps driving past it because the building has a storefront.

The back room is dimly lit with mattresses all around on the floor. They quickly close the door and take Alexis to one of the unoccupied mattresses and lay her on her back. Nancy leaves Anna with Alexis and other people in the room.

"I'm burning up!" Alexis exclaims.

Anna is trying to keep her calm, "You're okay."

Alexis starts to pull some of her clothes off, "I'm too hot."

Anna pats her forehead with a napkin as she admires Alexis's beauty. She kisses Alexis, "Shhhhh!!!"

"What is happening to me?" Alexis asks.

"Nothing, just keep calm. You'll be fine."

Billy walks in the room and yells, "Turn up time!"

Anna pulls away from Alexis as Billy stands over them. "You can go, Anna. I got it from here."

Anna moves away.

Billy unfastens his jeans, drop his underwear and grabs Alexis by her hair.

He pulls her face to his crotch and forces her to perform orally.

Anna exits the room.

Alexis is so high from mollies in her water that she has lost control. She is almost unconscious. When Billy pushes her back on the mattress she falls lifelessly.

"How do I taste you, thot?" Billy yells.

He zips up his pants, "Anybody want the prom queen?"

Billy turns and walks away. In an instant, a group of guys finish undressing Alexis. The guys have her naked as they take turns having sex with her one after another.

Travon spots someone he knows from school walking down the block and drives up on them, "Hey! Where's the party?" He gets direction from one of his classmates.

Travon parks and walks around the back with the students from the school. He could hear the music before he entered and once he went in it was on and Crack'in. The party is packed.

The bass pounds as Travon walks around looking for Alexis. He approaches Anna who is dancing in her bra and high out of her mind.

"You seen Alexis?" Travon asks.

Anna places her arms on Travon's shoulders trying to get him to dance, "Yep! I seen her. She busy now, though."

He gently removes Anna's arms from around his neck. "Where is she?"

"Don't worry about her. Billy gave her what she deserves."

Travon gets angry, "What is that supposed to mean?"

He grabs Anna's wrist tightly, "Where is she?"

"You're hurting me. Ouch! She's in the back! Now, let go Stupid Star. You're too late," Anna replies as she continues to dance.

Travon makes his way to the back of the building pushing passed people. He pauses when he gets to the door of the room in the back. He enters, "Alexis!

Alexis!!!" He reaches for a light switch as his eyes adjust to the darkness.

Alexis is very weak as she calls for him, "Tray!"

He runs over to the mattress where some random guy is having sex with her. Travon grabs him, "Get off her!" He pulls the guy off Alexis.

"Okay Dude, chill…." The guy replies.

"Get the hell out of here dude," Travon says, angrily, with a stern tone.

Travon falls to her side and grabs her clothing. She reaches for him with a faint voice, "Tray!" He quickly covers Alexis, putting her clothes on her before pulling her up to walk out the door.

At that moment, Travon realizes that Alexis has been drugged. She can't stand up. Travon sweeps her into his arms and rushes out the back door and down the alley to his car. He props her up against the car but she keeps tilting over.

Another person recognizes Alexis and comes to her aid.

Travon takes off. He goes back inside the party pushing his way aggressively through the crowd, catching people's attention. He confronts Billy pushing him in the chest with both hands.

Billy throws both hands in the air over his head, "Hold'em up Super Star, this is a party. Not a brawl."

Travon repeatedly shoves Billy. Billy just chills and giggles. He is high.

The music has stopped and everyone looks at the two of them. Travon, frustrated that Billy won't defend himself, turns to go back outside.

"Turn up!" Billy yells.

The music starts and people party like there's no tomorrow.

Outside, Eric couldn't keep Alexis conscious.

"What's up with her, bro?" Travon demands.

"I don't know, but mollies don't have you like this. Something else is going on. Alexis is sweating ridiculously."

Travon, opening the passenger door of his car, "Help me get her in the car."

Alexis's body falls limp as she slides down in the front seat of the car. He places the car in gear and speeds away.

Eric watches Travon as he accelerates swiftly away wondering what has just happened. He knows Alexis is in bad shape.

Travon pulls up quickly and parks the car. He grabs his phone and calls Carlos.

"What up, bro? I thought you were done with me?" Carlos answers jokingly.

Travon, speaking frantically, "Bro, come out and help me."

Carlos is serious, "What's going on, bro?"

Travon, out of breath, "It's Alexis, Dawg. Lexis, Billy got to her."

Inside the house, Lisa takes Alexis's temperature. "Her temp has gotten severe. Carlos, go run some cold water in the tub quickly," she says.

Travon is winded on the couch, in shock.

"Move, now!!!" Lisa yelled.

Carlos smacks Travon, "Snap out of it."

Travon just sits there nervously while Carlos runs the bath water. They get Alexis in the bathroom, remove her clothes and place her in the tub in her undershirt. Lisa turns on the shower splashing water in Alexis's face trying to get her temperature down. Lisa returns to the living room where Travon and Carlos discuss what happened.

"She should be okay now," Lisa says.

"What we need to do?" Travon asks.

"Let her rest and give her plenty of fluids."

"I can't believe this."

"She's resting in my bed. She'll be okay. Go home."

"That's bogus, dude!" Carlos says with a frown, "something has to be done about this."

Travon nods in agreement, "I'm out."

After Travon leaves, Lisa checks on Alexis to see if she is all right. She rushes out of the room screaming at Carlos, "Call 911! Alexis looks like she is in shock! Something is wrong!"

The ambulance comes immediately and gets her to the hospital.

At the hospital, Alexis is being rushed into an emergency room as the nurse checks her vital signs. She is in and out of consciousness with a very high fever.

The doctor comes quickly to her room frantically giving orders, "Start an IV. We need to get her temperature down immediately if we want to save this young lady. What's her name, Nurse Diaz?"

"Alexis Petitis," Nurse Diaz replies.

Dr. Smith grabs ice packs, placing them all over Alexis, "Does anyone know what happened to her?"

Nurse Diaz, "My daughter brought her in and said she got drugged by friends."

Dr. Smith smirks, "Friends, huh? We need to pump Alexis's stomach to see what she ingested. These darn kids just don't understand what they are doing to their bodies … smoking, drinking, pills, and Lord knows what else they're doing. Pass me the vacuum."

Chapter 11

The following Monday at school, Carlos runs into Travon by the locker room. He tells Travon that Lisa had to take Alexis to the emergency room because she had a high fever. Travon stands in disbelief as Billy walks up behind them.

"Man, that was one wild party Friday night," says Billy with a smirk on his face.

"Yeah, I guess so," says Travon, "Alexis ended up in the hospital."

"Oh well," says Billy, "she ain't nothing but a party girl or thot, whichever you prefer."

Carlos aggressively approaches, "Billy! If you had anything to do with that, man that's fucked up!"

Billy falls back laughing, "Well, Carlos, let's just say I took one for the team," shoving Carlos up off him, he turns and starts walking away.

"She's pressing charges on everybody involved," Travon says, catching Billy's attention.

Billy pauses and looks back over his shoulder at Carlos and Travon, "Ask Alexis how I taste and if they can get DNA out of her stomach?" He continues walking.

Travon rushes Billy, pushing him into the wall.

Coach Matthews, walking around the corner, "What the hell is going on here? Break it up."

"DNA on that Stupid Star!" Billy replies as he adjusts his backpack walking away.

"Travon what's going on here?" asks Coach Matthews.

"Nothing, Coach!" Carlos answers.

"GET YOUR BUTTS TO CLASS NOW!"

Travon, with a mean mug, walks away with Carlos on his heels.

"Billy going to get it, bro, don't trip," Carlos says.

Travon nods in agreement as they walk in the direction of class. He is furious. Carlos continues to try to calm Travon down.

Travon knocks on the history classroom door because he is late and enters the room.

"Welcome, Travon," says Ms. Johnson, "just because you're the captain of the team doesn't give you the right to come cruising up in my classroom late. Now have a seat and turn to page 128."

"Yes, Ma'am."

"Tray … Travon," Samantha tries to get Travon's attention. He is too angry and stares down at his history book.

"Ms. Samantha Stevens, is there something you would like to share with the class, young lady?" Ms. Johnson politely asks.

"No, Ms. Johnson."

Travon looks over at Samantha to ask, what's up? without speaking. Ms. Johnson pauses for a second and turns back to the chalkboard.

Samantha whispering to Travon, "What's up with my girl?"

Travon, unable to make out what Samantha is saying, turns toward the blackboard.

Ms. Johnson quickly turns around, "There should be no talking if I'm talking, Ms. Stevens."

Samantha sits up straight, with a shocked expression on her face, "Huh?"

"You'll be meeting with me today after school, Ms. Stevens. Bring all your belongings, you'll be dismissed from my classroom."

Samantha tries to respond, "I didn't…."

"Quiet, young lady, or you can step out of my classroom."

The entire classroom murmurs and giggles.

Samantha frowns, "Yes Ma'am."

Ms. Johnson continues to teach her lesson.

Chapter 12

That following week, Alexis returns to school as if nothing happened. It's prom week, and she looks just like the queen she'd been elected to be. During passing period, the halls are full. As Travon and Alexis pass one another, she grabs his hand and pulls him to the side.

"Hello, Tray! Thanks for your help. Lisa told me what you did for me," she kisses him on the cheek lightly.

Travon smiles, "Is that all I get after all the worrying you had me doing."

She speaks very sincerely, "That's all you want anyway."

"Why didn't you call me or text?" Travon asks.

"Didn't want to involve you in that whole ordeal with my parents, so I told Lisa not to tell you anything."

Alexis slightly squeezes Travon's hand, "You are the perfect gentleman. The average guy would have just taken advantage of me, but not you. You are a true friend, and thanks again." She releases his hand.

"You would have done the same for me."

"Yeah, I suppose I would have."

The bell sounds for the start of next period. They walk separate ways. Travon is looking over his shoulder at Alexis thinking, something has changed about her.

It's the sixth period. Alexis enters the lunchroom before all her friends make it there.

Darlene walks in screaming, "HEY BFF!"

Alexis smiles as Darlene gives her a big hug.

"Enough already," Alexis starts playfully pulling away from Darlene.

Tameika walks up teary eyed, "Are you okay?"

Alexis forces a smile, "Girl, I'm fine, can you tell?" She shakes her long hair back and forth, "I'm gucci, squad."

Samantha walks in very seriously and approaches Darlene, Tameika, and Alexis.

Alexis is concerned, "What's wrong with this chick?"

Darlene, unconcerned, "Ain't nothing wrong with that thot!"

"You so wrong for that," Alexis replies as they both laugh.

Samantha mimics them, "Hee hee ha ha! Screw both of you chicks."

Darlene, joyfully, "Don't come over here trying to ruin our moment." "Grrrr! Talk to the hand," Samantha replies.

"For real, what's going on with you?" Alexis asks.

"I got in trouble because of your butt," Samantha states. "Huh?"

"Inquiring about you last week got me after school detention."

Travon walks up at that moment, "Talking too much got you in trouble."

"I was checking up on my friend," Samantha responds.

Darlene laughs, "Yep! That's her, 'Ms. Talk a Lot.' Told you she should be a rapper."

They all laugh together as they grab their lunch trays. Travon looks at Alexis's plate, "No cheese fries today."

"Nope! Just healthy eating from here on out."

Travon, trying to loosen Alexis up, "Out where? Outback Steak House?" he jokes, "you've never eaten healthy."

"Maybe not, but I can try," she responds jokingly.

They sit together to eat and chat for a moment when the bell sounds. Samantha finishing her drink, says, "Dang! This period went by fast."

"They all do these days. Time just flies waiting for no one." Alexis states.

Travon thinks to himself that something about Alexis's behavior is different. They all walk to exit the cafeteria, Samantha still playing around with her drink.

"Hurry with that drink. You know Mall Cop not going to let you out of here with that drink," Darlene says.

"He's very handsome, though," Tameika expresses. They laugh.

"Yeah, he's always doing the most," Samantha replies, tossing her drink in the trash. They all depart heading to their respective classes.

Chapter 13

It's prom night, and Janice's parents are letting Travon drive their late model Caddy STS. The team has agreed to meet at Travon's mom's house so that they can all drive to the prom together.

Travon pulls up with Janice, exits and runs around to the passenger door to open it for her. Janice's dress is flawless and matches Travon's baby-blue tux as she steps out of the car.

Carlos and Lisa come out of Travon's house. They are stunning. Lisa is wearing a soft pink dress trimmed with red. It matches Carlos's red vest. They stand in front of Travon's house taking pictures with Mrs. Singleton.

The neighbors are out taking pictures, as well, when a late model 550 Mercedes Benz pulls up with tinted windows and catches everybody's attention. Everyone turns to see who's driving the Benz.

At the same moment, the trunk opens slowly, and the top begins to collapse back into the trunk. Billy steps out of the car looking like a million bucks as he steals the moment from Carlos and Travon.

Billy is rocking a mint-green tux. He is sharp. Anna, his date, is wearing a knee-length mint dress.

Seconds later, a white limo pulls up with the sunroof open and steals the thunder from Billy. It's Alexis and Cory.

Cory is the star basketball player from a rival school. Cory, tall, dark and handsome, plays the perfect gentleman as he walks around to open the door for Alexis. She pops out of the car looking the part of prom queen. She is wearing all white. She has everybody staring and admiring her.

Travon has a bitter look on his face. He is looking in Billy's direction as they all line up to take pictures for Mrs. Singleton. The flashes just keep flashing as everybody snaps away.

At that moment, Billy yells, "Hey! Take a picture of the king and queen?"

Alexis turns toward Billy, then toward Janice, "Janice do you mind if Travon and I take a picture?"

Janice, quite surprised by Alexis's manners smiles, "No, go right ahead."

As Alexis and Travon pose together, they chat.

"Tray, you and Janice are welcome to ride in the limo along with Cory and me," Alexis offers.

"Thanks, but I'd rather drive," He replies.

Carlos walks over, "Lex, you look great!"

"Thank you, Carlos. You're very handsome yourself." Alexis replies.

"Where's Benny and Robert?" Carlos asks.

Travon looks at his watch, "I'm not sure, but we out of here in ten minutes."

"I thought that we were all taking a team picture for your mom," Carlos says.

"We'll just have to take it at the prom," Travon responds.

They all group up for one last picture before getting back into their vehicles and heading to prom.

Travon pulls away slowly. Billy pulls off right behind them with the top down on that Benz. Carlos has his hand hanging out of the window, showing off his watch, slowly driving behind Billy. Alexis and Cory are standing out of the sunroof of the limo. People are videotaping and taking Instagram photos.

Chapter 14

At the prom, everyone is taking pictures and enjoying the moment. Darlene and Alexis are standing off to the side. Alexis compliments her friend, "Darlene your hair really looks nice."

"Thanks. Your date really looks nice," Darlene responds.

"What about me? "Alexis asks.

Darlene playfully starts laughing, "Oh, you too."

Samantha walks over hollering, "HEY!! OMG, You both look so beautiful."

Alexis smiles and steps back to take a good look at Samantha, "You look fabulous."

Samantha, being conceited, spins around slowly, "I do, don't I?"

"You're doing the most now, diva!" Darlene says.

Alexis's cell phone vibrates. She answers the call, "Hello!?"

Tameika, in a shallow toned voice, "Hello."

"Girl, where are you?"

"Still at home."

"WHAT? WHY?" Alexis yells.

"Because Rob's cousin decided at the last minute he couldn't use his car," Tameika starts crying, "so … so I don't have a ride."

Alexis quickly walks toward the exit, "Oh, you got a ride."

"Huh?" Tameika responds.

Alexis walks over to her limo. The chauffeur, who is standing outside smoking a cigar, inquires, "Yes, young lady? are you ready to leave?"

"Is it possible for you to pick up a friend who doesn't have a ride to the prom?"

"Yes, you have my services all night."

"Really?"

He puffs on his cigar and exhales, "Really!"

Alexis writes down the address and returns inside. Cory sees her and reaches for her hand. He stops Alexis in her tracks, "Is everything okay, PG?"

"I just had to help a friend," Alexis replies. "So, as long as you're cool, I'm gucci."

"You're a little too cool. What's got into you?"

Cory giggles, "Nothing." The big grin on his face reveals that great smile that he has.

"Give me a minute. I have to go talk to Darlene and Sam," Alexis declares as she walks away a little annoyed, "Lord!"

"Where the hell did you go?" Darlene asks.

"While you were gone, Cory and Billy were chatting and giggling like girls," Samantha says.

Alexis crosses her arms, "Really?"

At that moment, Tameika walks into prom without a date. She is wearing a red spaghetti strap dress that meets her knee on one leg and her thigh on the other. Instantly, everybody turns to look at her. Darlene, Sam, and Alexis quickly move in her direction. They all hug. Alexis is the last to hug her.

Tameika whispers in Alexis's ear, "Thanks!"

Alexis whispers back, "I love you girl."

Tameika gets a little misty-eyed. She regains her composure and they start to dance. Samantha yells, "Squad!"

The music stops. The D.J. speaks,

"Testing one, two, three…. Okay people, the king and queen are about to be crowned."

Everybody admires how good Alexis and Travon look together as they are crowned on the stage. Cameras just keep flashing, taking pictures of couples around the room. Alexis takes in the moment and leans over toward Travon, "Get used to this, Super Star. This is your future."

Travon smiles and waves at the crowd, "Whatever."

The DJ turns on a slow song and Travon and Alexis leave the stage to dance together. Cory and Janice dance nearby before switching partners.

The banquet hall is perfect for the occasion with finger-foods and beverages arranged beautifully. Students sip on soda and eat as they chat about their plans for the following day.

The prom has ended and everyone is headed for downtown Chicago. They're going to the Buckingham Fountain. The lighting of the fountain sets the mood for photos and cuddling.

Carlos and Lisa, along with Travon and Janice, take a group picture before heading for a walk downtown.

The other students head for home and other places.

Travon and Janice are having a great time when a horse and carriage pulls directly in front of them. Alexis and Cory are inside the carriage.

Carlos with a hint of excitement, "That's, what's up?"

Lisa smiles, "Yeah, that's cool."

Alexis pushes the door of the carriage open, "Get in!" Janice frowns.

Carlos steps up in the carriage reaching behind to grab Lisa's hand. Carlos reaches back grabbing Janice's hand.

She still frowns as Carlos pulls her aboard.

Travon climbs on and sits next to Alexis. Cory, Carlos, and Travon start to talk about hoops as all the girls chime in.

Alexis keeps catching Janice staring at her. She tries to assure Janice that she's good with Cory. She cuddles closer to him. Cory reaches around her pulling her even closer to him.

"What happened to Robert?"

Carlos looks at Travon, "Yeah, bro!"

"I'm not really sure," Travon answers.

Alexis ponders on the thought of telling them but instead she decides to change the subject, "It's such a beautiful night to be riding down the Magnificent Mile."

"It sure is," Lisa replies in agreement.

The carriage ride has ended with talks of tomorrow's agenda. The couples are separating, going their respective ways. They embrace with hugs before departing. Cory and Alexis are hugging as they walk off.

"So, what's this Billy was saying about you and some dude named Big Randy?" Cory asks Alexis.

Alexis stops in her tracks, "Big Randy is nobody in my book. He plays on the football team and is good for nothing."

"Did you ever date him?" Cory asks.

"No, we went to a movie together. Besides that, I don't really care what Billy told you, but this ain't that!"

Cory is feeling the negative energy, "Whoa Shorty. I'm just asking." He reaches to put his arm around Alexis, and they continue to walk.

Lisa and Carlos walk in the opposite direction once Alexis calms down.

Janice and Travon stand and embrace while sharing a really long passionate kiss. They walk back to the car. Travon drops Janice off at home. They discuss plans for the amusement park tomorrow.

The next day all the students meet at the school to drive to the humongous amusement park in Milwaukee.

At the park, they stand in line for an hour waiting to get on the most enormous roller coaster in the Midwest. They get to the front of the line and the girls are having a change of heart. The guys talk them into getting on the ride. Screams can be heard all over the amusement park. The rollercoaster pulls back up and the girls' hair is all over their heads. The guys get off laughing at the girls who are screaming bloody murder. They exit the ramp and begin walking over to play games.

Carlos, Travon, and Cory all walk over to the hoops game. The fellas begin shooting baskets and winning stuffed animals for their dates. Cory has won the largest stuffed animal for Alexis and Travon tries to outshoot Cory at hoops … with no such luck.

They all continue to enjoy the rest of the evening and get on as many rides as possible before nightfall. Most of the students are exhausted as they walk toward the exit. Alexis let the top down on her Mustang to get her stuffed animal in the car. As they all race back home, they all part ways jumping off at different exit ramps heading home.

Travon pulls up in front of Janice's home as she sleeps inside the car. He wakes her with a kiss. She's groggy trying to figure out where they are, "Where are we?"

"At your parents' house," Travon says.

Janice smirks, "Why are we here? I'm going home with you."

Travon laughs, "Whatever! You play too much." Janice lies back on the seat closing her eyes.

"Oh, this is that?" Travon asks.

"Yes, it is. Now drive," Janice orders with a smile and nodding her head.

Travon immediately drives away headed home. As they pull in front of Travon's house, Janice is knocked out sleep. He puts the car in park, leans over and kisses Janice on the lips. She awakens with a smile. She steps out of the car with Travon walking behind her. He is admiring her shapely body.

She peeps back at Travon, "Why are you watching me like that?"

"No reason," He says as he inserts the key in the door.

Janice looks around as if it's her first time in Travon's house, "Where is Momma Singleton?"

"Oh, she's working an overnight shift."

"Okay."

They both enter Travon's bedroom. Janice grabs the remote control to turn on the television. She lies back on the bed.

"I'm going to take a quick shower," Travon says.

Jokingly, Janice replies, "Smells like a good idea … you stink!"

He removes his T-shirt and smells his underarms, "YOU LIE!" playfully throwing his shirt at her.

She admires Travon's six-pack and mocha-colored skin. He exits the room and heads to the shower. The bathroom door is cracked open. Janice turns the sound down and listens to the shower running. She gets up and starts to undress with her heart pounding in her chest from excitement and fear.

At that moment, Janice is not sure if she wants to lose her virginity. She slowly creeps down to the bathroom and slides her hand into the room. She cuts off the light.

Travon screams playfully, "I'm scared!! Please don't hurt me."

Janice moves over to the shower. She's naked. She sticks her hand behind the shower curtain without him noticing. She grabs his butt.

Travon laughs, "Freaky, freaky…, freaky!!!" as he continues washing up.

She steps in the shower. He turns towards her and reaches for her hand so that she doesn't slip. They embrace one another before they start to kiss.

Travon's heart races because he has never been this close to Janice. He whispers in her ear, "Are you sure about this?"

She places her finger on his lips and nods affirmatively. She kisses him deeply. He grabs the towel and gently washes her body. He exits the shower and grabs towels as they head to his bedroom.

Travon, caught off guard, is not prepared. He does not have a condom. He rambles through his dresser looking for a condom. Janice reaches over to her purse and pulls out a prophylactic.

The next morning Travon's mom comes up to his room. "TRAY!!" She knocks then enters.

"Hey, Mom!"

"Good morning, Momma Singleton!" Janice says.

They're both on top of the covers, fully dressed and watching T.V.

Mrs. Singleton is surprised, "Hey, sweetheart. Travon, downstairs now!"

A look of worry strikes her face as she walks away. Travon slides out of bed quickly to follow his mom downstairs.

Janice is alarmed by the tone of Mrs. Singleton's voice. She could hear the conversation between Tray and his mom. She gathers her things together.

Travon returns to the room all smiles, "Why are you getting your things?"

"I heard your mom's tone."

"Don't even trip. She's gucci." Travon says.

Chapter 15

That following Monday after prom, some students are cleaning out their lockers. Alexis approaches Travon from behind and places her hands over his eyes.

The smell of her perfume gives her away. "Alexis!" Travon yells.

She removes her hands, "How did you know it was me?"

He turns toward her, "I know that smell anywhere."

Alexis is looking cute as usual. He turns back to his locker and continues straightening it out.

"Tray, Anna said that she heard that I was pressing charges against all who were involved. You wouldn't know anything about that?"

Travon glances over his shoulder, "Not at all."

"I'm sure you don't," Alexis replies.

"It would serve them well if that happens anyway."

Students pass by and speak, "Hey, Tray! Hey, Lex!"

Tray and Alexis both speak very nonchalantly, "Hey!"

"I know you were the one who said I would be pressing charges, but it's cool," Alexis states.

She pauses for a second, "Tray, I never thought I'd say this. You and Janice make a good couple."

"What???"

"She's a very nice person."

Travon turns and looks Alexis in her eyes, "And who said maturity doesn't come overnight, huh?"

Alexis smiles, "Thanks for everything again." She reaches up to hug Travon and kisses him on the cheek before turning to walk away.

Travon grabs his bag out of his locker with a big grin on his face. He closes his locker.

He then sees Janice a few feet from him. She's walking with Valarie. Janice gives him a hard stare, "What was that, Tray?"

"Well, hello to you, sweetie," he says as he tries to lean over and kiss her on the cheek. Janice frowns and walks away with Valarie.

Valarie looks back at Travon, "Later, Stupid Star."

Travon starts to walk behind them and stops because Janice is extremely upset. He thinks to himself, better let her cool off. He slams his locker in frustration.

Janice and Valarie proceed down the corridor without looking back. "I told you him and that thot was up to something," Valarie states.

Janice is upset, "Please let's not even talk about it. It's Senior Cut Week, and I plan on surprising him, and this is what I get?"

Valarie pauses before speaking as Janice wipes away a tear from her eye. "Sorry I invited you," Valarie says.

Janice rushes to a nearby restroom and breaks down once she gets inside.

Valarie tries to comfort her as she dresses for gym class.

Travon heads over to Coach Matthews office. He knocks on the door. "Come in."

Travon enters.

"Hey, Travon! What's going on young man?"

Travon takes a seat, "What's to women?"

Coach Matthews smiles, "Well, son, all women are different and yet quite the same."

Travon looks confused, "What, Coach?"

"I mean, they all want the same things, but at different times."

Travon looks puzzled, "Are you talking about you or me? Because I'm not following."

"Let's just say you'll experience all you need to know about women in time."

"Thanks, coach I have to get to class."

"You're welcome, son. Come back, anytime."

Travon turns away from Coach Matthews. Confused, he thinks to himself, *What the hell*?

Coach Matthews sits in his chair laughing then speaks aloud, "You will figure it all out. It's called 'growing pains'."

Travon, on the way to class, is not responsive to other students speaking to him.

"Hey, King Tray," someone says.

Travon doesn't even acknowledge the compliment.

That following week is Janice's Senior Prom. Travon keeps trying to make contact with Janice but with no luck. He calls. He texts. He even stops by her parents' house. On one occasion Janice's father opens the door and tells him that Janice is not there, but Travon can see her behind the door.

Travon feels rejected and calls Alexis while he lies on his bed.

Alexis answers with a faint voice, "Hello!"

"Hey, babe!"

Alexis knows who it is and plays him off, "Who is this?"

Travon, even more in his feelings, says, "It's me."

"Me, who? Don't call here playing on my phone." She hangs up on Travon.

Travon looks at his cell phone like the call dropped, but he knows that Alexis has hung up.

Tray jumps up out his bed and rushes downstairs when he hears his mom come in the door. He rushes over and takes the bags of groceries out of her hand, giving her a big kiss.

"Boy, what has gotten into you?"

"Nothing, Mom. I just love you so much."

"I love you, too, Son. Now, what's going on?" She takes a seat at the table and listens to Travon's situation about Janice.

"Hmmm! Maybe I should give her a call."

She calls Janice.

Janice looks at the caller I.D. and hands it to her father. He answers with a deep voice, "Hello!"

"Hello! Is Janice available? This is Mrs. Singleton, Travon's mom."

"Oh, hey, Mrs. Singleton. This is Janice's dad. If you're calling about prom, Janice has elected to go with her cousin. I apologize for any inconvenience this may cause, so please understand."

Mrs. Singleton is shocked, "Oh, okay. You have a great evening."

"Bye!"

"Bye!"

Travon eagerly waits to hear what was said, "Okay, what did he say?"

She explains the highs and lows of life as Travon's eyes get watery. She embraces her son.

How upset is Travon being torn between two girls? Evidently, he cares a lot about Alexis and still wants Janice to be his girl.

Chapter 16

It's summer vacation and Janice hasn't spoken to Travon since the day at the lockers. Valarie made sure that Janice knew about the rumors circling Travon and Alexis's sexual encounter.

Travon is at home with Carlos looking over pamphlets from several different colleges as they both prepare for their senior year. Carlos and Travon joke about what the girls would be like once they get to college. Travon pauses, "Dang, I still have not gotten a call back from Janice or a return text."

"Don't sweat it, bro. She'll come around. It just takes time." Carlos assures him.

Travon laughs, "Look at you. When did you become the love doctor?"

"I'm not the love doctor … I'm Doctor Love!" Carlos stands like he's a superhero with his hands on his hips.

Both of them start laughing hysterically. Travon pushes Carlos down on the couch, "Sit down. You're crazy, bro."

Travon's smartphone beeps. He looks down to check his message. It's a text from Alexis. It reads, I really need to talk with you. It's of great importance. N2U

"It's Lexis, she already done enough," Travon says.

"Remember, bro … what she's been through," Carlos reminds him.

"I know, but I didn't cause that. Did I?"

Carlos, with a stern tone, "Nope! But it still happened."

"You right. You really are a doctor, huh? Get yo wannabe Doctor Frankenstein looking…."

They both start laughing. Travon returns Alexis's text, HEY ALEXIS, WHAT'S UP?

She replies immediately, I THOUGHT WE AGREED THAT WE WOULD BE FRIENDS.

NOW IS THE TIME I NEED ONE THE MOST. N2U

Travon becomes angry thinking back to how she caused Janice to leave him alone. He responds angrily, DON'T KNOW WHAT YOU'RE GOING THROUGH, NOR DO I REALLY CARE. JUST LEAVE ME ALONE. NOT INTO YOU.

Alexis never replies.

Travon tells Carlos what he just texted to Alexis.

Carlos is not cool with the text, "Bro, Alexis is still good peeps. That was bogus, you took it to that level with her. It was all gucci, then."

Travon gives Carlos a strange look, "Whatever!"

* * *

Weeks later, Travon is at the drugstore with his mother when he runs into Alexis's parents, The Petitises.

Alexis's parents approach Travon, "Excuse me, young man," her mom, Mrs. Petitis, says, "don't I know you from the prom pictures you took with my daughter Alexis."

Travon very politely extends his hand, "Yes, ma'am." They all greet one another.

"Is it possible that I can speak with you for a moment?" asks Mrs. Petitis.

Mrs. Singleton walks up concerned, "What about?"

"Mom! These are Alexis's parents, meet The Petitis family."

"Nice to meet you," Mrs. Singleton exclaims.

"We wanted to speak to you about Alexis," Mrs. Petitis's eyes start to tear up.

Travon instantly becomes concerned, "Is she okay?"

"I'm afraid not," answers Mr. Petitis, "we knew our daughter liked the party scene but never thought it would…."

Tears instantly stream down his face. He's unable to finish the conversation and abruptly walks out of the store.

The store P.A. system sounds, "Mrs. Petitis, Mr. Green, Mrs. Singleton, YOUR PRESCRIPTION IS READY FOR PICK UP."

Mrs. Singleton and Mrs. Petitis proceed back to the counter to purchase their items.

Travon follows Alexis's dad out to the parking lot. He taps on the car window on the passenger side of the car, and Mr. Petitis pops the locks. Travon gets in the car. Travon is curious about what's going on as he looks at Mr. Petitis, a big man in size who does not appear to shake easily.

Mr. Petitis's eyes are red from crying but he holds back his tears long enough to say, "My baby has contracted AIDS," he bursts out into tears again.

Travon, having all kinds of mixed emotions, doesn't know how to respond. His eyes fill with tears in disbelief as his heart pounds in his chest. He thinks back to how he treated Alexis when she tried to contact him.

Travon is feeling badly, "Would it be okay if I came over?"

Mr. Petitis, fighting back his tears, "That would be fine."

Mrs. Petitis opens the passenger door to let Travon out of the car. He gives her a big hug, "Tell Alexis that I'll be over."

"Okay, young man, I'll tell her," Mrs. Petitis says.

Travon gets in the car with his mom as The Petitis family drives away honking the horn.

"That is truly sad," Mrs. Singleton says with grief.

"She told you about Alexis, huh?" Travon asks.

On the drive home Mrs. Singleton grows concerned. "Tray, you didn't have sex with that girl. Did you?"

"No, Mom, I didn't."

"I know you're protecting yourself if you did, right?"

Travon is slightly embarrassed, "Mom, yes."

"I know you light up like a bulb when Alexis's name comes up, so I'm just checking."

Travon tries to convince her, "I'm fine, Mom. Really."

As they drive home, Travon's mind drifts back to the night Alexis performed oral sex on him. He gets very nervous at that moment.

"Tray, what is that expression on your face about?" Mrs. Singleton asks.

Travon is trying to deflect the question, "I'm gucci, Mom."

"Gucci, huh? I don't want you to get caught up out here? Better be sure that you practice safe sex."

"Yes, Ma'am."

Chapter 17

A couple of days later, Travon is sitting outside of Alexis's residence trying to build up his courage to go inside. Finally, he gets out of the car. He rings the bell giving himself a look over to make sure his gear is on point. Mrs. Petitis opens the door with a smile and invites Travon inside. Alexis is sitting on the couch covered with a blanket watching T.V. Travon walks in with flowers and lays them on the table in front of Alexis. He sits on the loveseat across from her. Alexis giggles.

"What's so funny?"

"You! It's okay if you come over and sit by me. You can only get it from sexual intercourse or sharing needles."

He gets up and takes a seat right next to her, "You sure don't look sick."

"Thanks!"

She goes on to explain that she has full-blown AIDS, and it's just a matter of time before it takes over her body. He asks her where she thought she had contracted AIDS. She says she believes that it happened at Fat Freddie's party the night she had been drugged. She goes on to explain how everybody thought that she was The Party Girl when in fact she was the opposite.

"So where did the rumor come from?" Travon questions.

"Big Randy."

"Big Randy on the football team?"

"Yep, He went around telling people that he and I had slept together while his brother watched."

"DANG! And Big Randy seems like a cool guy. Wow, you blew me with that one."

"Blew you, huh? Really?"

"You know what I mean."

"Anyhow, that's where The Party Girl came from … Big Randy and them guys. Then at prom, Billy with his bean-head self, told Cory the story like it was true or something."

Travon is speechless. Finally he says, "Wow! That's deep."

"Creeps!" Alexis exclaims.

"Why didn't you confront him?"

"I did. Big Randy just lied and said his little brother started the rumor. Another lie. Why would Big Randy care if it made him look cool in his friends' eyes?"

"That's bogus!" Travon replies.

She reaches over and grabs Travon's hand, "It didn't even matter to my real friends like you and my squad. You, Samantha, Tameika, and Darlene have stood by me regardless of the rumors."

Travon squeezes Alexis's hand to comfort her as her emotions take over. A tear forms in her eye and Travon quickly embraces her.

Alexis's parents stood around the corner listening to the stories that they never knew. Mrs. Petitis cries while Mr. Petitis holds her tightly not knowing when or what hour Alexis will die.

Travon is about to leave and then leans over to give Alexis another big hug and kiss on the cheek. She smiles and gets up to walk Travon to the door. Travon is devastated. He holds back his tears and stands at the door. They embrace again.

Travon, with a weak voice, "If you need anything call me. Don't hesitate."

Alexis, with a soft voice, moves closer to Travon, "Yeah, I need for you to tell everyone who you think was involved to get tested because someone is surely walking around with HIV."

Travon slightly confused, "If they have HIV, why do you have AIDS?"

Alexis explains, "My white blood cell count is low and couldn't fight off the virus attacking my body. Most people have a high white cell blood count that helps to fight off infections."

Travon can't grasp it all at once.

Alexis opens up the door for Travon to exit. Travon steps out on the front porch and looks back, "I'll talk to you later."

Alexis forces a smile, "Okay, Super Star."

Travon gets in the car, starts it up and before he can pull away he bursts out in tears. The thought of 'his Alexis' dying begins to trouble him.

In the house, Alexis returns to the couch where her parents are waiting. They all cry together and hold one another while feelings of despair hover over them. Alexis has never cried before that moment.

Weeks later, over the summer, Alexis passes away. The church is filled with family and friends. Mr. and Mrs. Petitis take it hard. They both sit in the front row as everyone passes the casket. Alexis looks like a princess wearing all white. She appears as if she is sleeping. Weeping can be heard all over the church as people break down. Darlene and Samantha come without Tameika. Samantha approaches the casket and sees her friend lying there. She collapses right at the casket. Darlene is no help to Samantha because she walks away too quickly.

Samantha's screams are bone-chilling, "NO … NOT MY BESTIE? NO … NO.… OH, MY GOD, NOT MY LEX!"

Onlookers try to pick Samantha up with no luck. She cries as she lies right there.

Mrs. Petitis gets out of her seat and goes over and extends her hand to Samantha. Samantha grabs Mrs. Petitis's hand. She kneels and pulls Sam off the floor.

They both stand by the casket embracing one another as others pass by to view the body. Darlene is outside being consoled by friends and family.

Mrs. Singleton and Travon approach the crowd of people. Travon starts crying before even reaching the church. Darlene glances over at Travon unable to speak. He turns back around not wanting to go inside.

"Son, I'll go inside and pay my respects. You don't have to come in. You can just remember her the way she was." Mrs. Singleton says.

Travon just nods as he fights away his tears. Carlos and Lisa come out of the church speaking to no one as Lisa consoles Carlos.

Travon goes back to the car and waits for his mom to return. He cries like a newborn in the car.

Moments later, the church starts to clear out and the pallbearers carry the casket down the stairs of the church.

Travon steps back outside of the car and places his hand on his heart, saying to himself, "Goodbye my friend." He breaks down in tears. His mom rushes over to his side. She puts him back into the car.

Tameika stays at the house for the repast. She helps others to prepare for the return of the family. She hadn't gotten over the loss of a family friend and couldn't bring herself to attend the funeral.

Chapter 18

It's the first day of school. Over the summer students had learned about Alexis's sudden death. The counselor's office had set up a makeshift memorial for Alexis on the main hallway bulletin board. There are pictures of Alexis in her cheerleader uniform, class pictures from freshman, sophomore and junior year along with her obituary.

The school monitor shows the halftime show of the championship game. Alexis was the captain. She stood out front. The video starts with Alexis and the cheerleader squad in the middle of the court.

"WE ARE THE BEST WOO…. FORGET THE REST WOO…."

The other cheerleaders join in with the chant. "YES. WE ARE THE BEST WOO FORGET THE REST WOO…."

They move in unison, side-to-side, clapping at the same time. They repeat the same chant. Alexis jumps up in the air landing in a full split. The video freezes at that moment. The screen reads rest in peace.

Students cry as they pass to pick up their school schedules. The cheerleader squad takes it the hardest. Some of them refuse to believe that Alexis isn't going to be captain of the team.

The basketball team comes in as one to pay their respects. Carlos and Travon are the only upperclassmen left, outside of Billy and Benny.

Carlos wipes away his tears and glances towards the central office. He taps Travon on the shoulder, "Yo, Tray, there is Benny with his parents."

Travon turns looks in the office to see Benny. Benny didn't acknowledge their presence as he looked right at them.

Later that day, in the locker room Travon overhears Benny has transferred for his senior year to a school up north. Rumor surrounding Alexis's death has it that someone informed the police about that night at the party. Fat Freddie has been picked up for questioning, and many remain unnamed. The investigation has everyone shook up.

Basketball season has rolled back around, and the team is in the locker room. Travon remains captain of the team. He dedicates the season to Alexis's memory, with an armband that reads "PG 13" The Party Girl. Coach Matthews calls the players out of the locker room.

Just before Travon walks out, some players approached him.

Henry tells Travon that he had been tested for HIV and is HIV-positive, but the strange thing is that his friend Travis had also slept with Alexis that same night and is HIV-negative. Travon is really confused and is trying to make sense of it all.

Travon asks, "So what are you saying?"

Henry takes a deep breath, "What I'm saying is that night at the Rave, I was with Alexis in that back room. When Billy finished with her Travis was next, then Benny, I went right after Benny."

Travon shows no emotion toward Henry. He thinks to himself, whatever happens, happens.

Henry sees Travon is unfazed by his guilt to tell someone, "It's Benny who is spreading the virus."

Across town, at Benny's new school, Benny is at the free-throw line preparing to shoot his first shot of the year for his new school team. He makes the basket.

THE END

EPILOGUE

Travon and the Condors took City that year, losing State. He and Janice remained friends even after she noticed that Travon had real feelings for Alexis.

The school launched an investigation into Alexis's death. The police got involved and labelled Alexis's death a homicide.

At Benny's school, rumors started to circulate about him having HIV, and his parents pulled him out and transferred him to a suburban school.

Travon went on to college for one year before declaring for the NBA draft. Travon donated fifteen percent of his signing bonus to AIDS awareness. Travon founded The Wrap IT Up Safe Sex Foundation in Alexis's memory. He went on to buy his mom a new home. He always kept in touch with Alexis's parents, sending game tickets and speaking with them often.

It's game time and the announcer calls Travon's name.

He bursts through his teammates taking center court. He tears open his armband with PG 13 on it then slowly rolls it up his arm as if it were a condom, reminding all to Wrap It Up! The whistle blows, and the game starts.

In some cases, you don't get a second chance.

Coming Soon- The Movie,
"The Party Girl"

THE PARTY GIRL QUESTIONNAIRE

1. WHO BETRAYED WHOM?

2. WHO WAS A TRUE FRIEND? EXPLAIN.

3. WHAT PART MIGHT ABSTINENCE HAVE PLAYED?

4. WHERE DID THE CONFLICT ORIGINATE?

5. WHAT SITUATION SPAWNED ALEXIS'S REPUTATION?

6. WHICH COUPLE HAD THE HEALTHIEST RELATIONSHIP? EXPLAIN.

7. SHOULD TRAVON HAVE BEEN MORE HONEST ABOUT ALEXIS? EXPLAIN.

8. SHOULD THE AUTHORITIES HAVE BEEN NOTIFIED?

9. WHO WAS MOST LIKELY TO HAVE TIPPED OFF THE POLICE?

10. WHAT LESSONS CAN BE LEARNED FROM THIS STORY?

11. WHICH CHARACTERS ARE MOST LIKELY TO REMAIN LIFELONG FRIENDS?

12. WHAT IS THE MOST IMPORTANT
    COMPONENT OF A RELATIONSHIP?

13. WHAT'S MORE IMPORTANT BETWEEN
    TRUST AND RESPECT?

14. HOW WILL THIS STORY HELP YOU AS YOU
    MOVE FORWARD IN LIFE?

15. WHAT PART DID DRUGS PLAY?

16. WHAT ROLE DID UNDERAGED DRINKING
    PLAY?

17. HOW DOES FAMILY PLAY A PART IN THIS
    STORY?

18. HOW WOULD YOU HAVE HANDLED THE
    SITUATION IF YOU WERE TRAVON?

19. HOW WOULD YOU HAVE HANDLED IT IF
    YOU WERE BILLY?

20. HOW WOULD YOU HAVE HANDLED IT IF
    YOU WERE ALEXIS?

These questions, along with more, will appear on a blog to compare and contrast the most common answers. This will allow students to compare answers and observe other perspectives.

Author's Bio

Kevin Whitaker was born in Chicago and raised in a small urban community, LeClaire Courts. His life experiences coupled with great writing skills spawned the release of his debut story, TPG - THE PARTY GIRL. His vision is to blend entertainment and education.

To schedule Kevin for a book reading at your next youth event and for more info.
email: Books@McClurePublishing.com.

www.ingramcontent.com/pod-product-compliance
Lightning Source LLC
Chambersburg PA
CBHW071000120726
47910CB00004B/1312